Christmas in the Wylder County Jail

by

Nicole McCaffrey
and
Kim Turner

The Wylder West

Christmas in the Wylder County Jail

Cover Art by *Tina Lynn Stout*

The Wild Rose Press, Inc.
PO Box 708
Adams Basin, NY 14410-0708
Visit us at www.thewildrosepress.com

Publishing History
First Edition, 2021
Trade Paperback ISBN 978-1-5092-4114-9
Digital ISBN 978-1-5092-4115-6

The Wylder West
Published in the United States of America

He glanced at the drink again. One small glass at a time or the whole bottle…it mattered little…Addie was right. He was no longer the man he even thought himself to be. Hell, he wasn't the same man as clear back to Sarah. And he'd loved her with all his heart, the same heart that broke when she'd chosen his brother Rick.

He'd left Wylder out of necessity, letting his brother raise the son that by rights belonged to him. But the shredding of his heart had come much later when he'd lost his second wife and daughter to a fire while out hunting. He hadn't been drinking then, not even a little—and look what had happened.

He wrapped his fingers around the small glass and with the other ground out the butt of the cigar. He'd buried his wife and later his brother, though nothing had come close to the pain of placing his small daughter in the ground. He pushed the glass aside once more, the bronze drink the one thing between him and the hurt that never ceased.

But Addie. Her touch brought a calm to the storms inside his heart and eased his mind. This time, he'd seen it in her precious blue eyes. He'd gone too far. Something lost, hidden behind disappointment if he were guessing. She was done and he damn well knew it. The decision was now his to make…the bottle or Addie.

Praise for Nicole McCaffrey and Kim Turner

"What happens when a city girl goes to the Wild West to help her mother, after her mother becomes injured? Well, let's just say it's not a nunnery she ends up visiting. Ohhh, and the doctor in that town will even make a city girl swoon!"

~*Regina, Net Galley Reviews*
~*~

"*WILD TEXAS WIND* is an excellent story with a spitfire heroine, a great hero, and a wonderful, slightly humorous climax."

~*Romantic Times*

~*~

"Should a man raised to be true to his moral code stand by and watch a woman he loves take off for the Dakotas with some slick-suited fortune hunter? The answer is worth turning the pages for. On a scale of 1-5 *WYLDER HEARTS* deserves a 5!"

~*Kat Henry Doran, Wild Women Reviews*
~*~

"Bravo for *DAWSON'S HAVEN*. Kim Turner is the master writer, combining the grit of cowboy life with the passion and courtship of the strong-willed heroine."

~*Jane Lewis, author of Home in Wylder*

Dedication

For all the readers who fell in love
with Russ and Miss Addie and wanted their story.

~

And in memory of our friend, Alex Christle.
We wouldn't have Wylder without you.

Acknowledgments

Much thanks to our editor Kaycee John for her fantastic editing.

And special thanks to Tina Lynn for our beautiful cover!

Prologue

Wylder, Wyoming, 1879

Russ Holt held Addie tighter as her body gave into the pleasure of their joining. She sighed as she clung to him; the only time he could ever be sure she belonged to him. Not that he needed any kind of reassurance. He rocked into her again and when the slightest cry escaped her throat, he found his own sweet release. She held him as he shuddered through, whispering her name.

Rolling from her, he tucked her into his arms and pulled her across his chest. He ran his fingers through the long blonde locks that smelled of the flower-scented perfume she sometimes wore. Loving Adelaide Willowby was always perfection and as much as her body could break him as a man, he needed the warmth of her voice in conversation just as often.

"You've been drinking again," she whispered as she ran her fingers through the hairs on his chest. Though she didn't move, her annoyance at the one habit he'd never left behind, the one demon he couldn't seem to fight or put behind him, was clear.

"Not drunk," he answered. Neither did he raise his own voice as he touched her cheek with a thumb.

She lifted her head to gaze into his face "Russ, Doc says it's bad for ya. Even just sippin'. I'm not gonna

1

stand by and watch you kill yourself with that bottle."

"Addie, let's...ahhh, damn it." He pushed the covers back and grabbing his trousers, rose. He wanted her, the touch of her body, and her voice—but not the scolding.

"Now you're gonna run right outta here because I call it like I see it." She said it with a hint of the pout that always made him smile. His Addie would put him out before morning anyway. She never let him spend the full night when he had been sippin' the liquor.

"Ain't runnin'. Got work to do." He turned to face her as he tugged on his shirt, leaving it open as he walked back to her. Leaning down, he placed his broad hands on the mattress and kissed her. "I'll ask you again. Marry me, Addie. Give me a reason to be in your bed each and every night, talkin' or lovin'."

She pushed him back before standing to pull a silken robe around her petite frame. He stood there, admiring until she was covered before tugging her into his arms again. "Come on, Addie, I ask you over and over and you never answer the question. And I've had a nip but not a lot."

She moved to the mirror to run a brush through her hair. "Russell, I've a business to run and no time for a marriage." That was his Addie, always minding her work except for a moment ago when she'd let herself go with him.

God, if he didn't love her so much, it wouldn't hurt to know he'd never be deserving of her. She was smart and beautiful and damn near took his breath every time he looked at her. But it seemed the one thing she asked was the one hardest for him to give up.

She turned, hairbrush at her shoulder. "Russ, you

have to do something about the drinking."

He sucked in a deep breath and turned away to look out the small window of the upper floor of The Wylder County Social Club. "Sober up, you mean."

She flipped the brush through her hair again. "Yes, and for good, not just a few days."

He gave a short grunt of disgust. When he wasn't in her arms, sober came with its own ghosts.

"Russell, I am not saying it will be easy, but Coyote says you have to back off...you can't keep this up." She turned him around to face her. "You must try. For us."

"Us?" He shook his head and lifted a thumb to wipe the tear from her cheek. "Ain't no *us*...I've asked you time and again to marry me and I'm gonna keep asking, but...we've made little progress there."

"There can't be us until you put the bottle behind you for good. I'm making no promises," she whispered, clinging to his open shirt. "But for now, you get dressed and get on outta here. I got work to do and mornin' comes early. You need to think about this, though, like I am saying."

He grimaced. He didn't want to cause her more pain than she'd already been through in her own life. "Hell, I don't know. I drink to forget. I drink to remember. But I never wanted to hurt you."

Addie grabbed his face with both hands. "Russ, look at me...look at me." She waited until he found her. "Let me be the reason you can put that bottle away for good. I can't ask for more than that. I'm here for you but I can't do it for you...no one can." She kissed his cheek. "You have to do that. You."

He listened to the silence between them, the tender

3

words she offered. No matter his attempts, he'd never been able to let go of the liquor. It was the one thing that numbed him when his mind wouldn't rest, when the pictures of the past stepped back in and he heard the sweet voices long gone.

And no matter Addie's wishes and no matter his love for her…the bottle still called.

Chapter One

Wylder, Wyoming, December 1879

"Russ Holt, a promise written on a block'a ice in August would last longer than one that come outta your mouth!" Adelaide Willowby gave the tall, lanky rancher a shove toward the door. "And this time, don't come back with your sweet-talkin' ways."

"But Addie—"

"Abraham!" she yelled at the top of her lungs. Where on earth was that bouncer when she needed him? She turned, unable to bear the stricken look on the cowboy's face a moment longer. "Abra—"

"Here, Miz Addie." Her hired man, who kept the patrons in check and protected the girls, emerged from the kitchen.

She pointed behind her. "Out. I want him *out!*"

A wince crossed his handsome dark face as he looked at the man in question and shrugged. "Sorry, Mister Holt, but she's the boss."

"I just want to es'plain," came the slurred response.

Noting the hesitancy in Abraham's dark gaze Addie released a huff of frustration. "If you won't do it, I'll get my rifle."

"I don't wanna hurt you, Mister Holt," Abraham sputtered. "Go'n now, nice and peaceful til she calm down."

"Calm down, my ass." Anger roiling, Addie stalked off. Another promise made; another promise broken. Men were all the same. Even the good ones.

The click of the latch on the front door brought her up short. For a moment, grief threatened to overwhelm her. Tears stung at her eyes. Had she expected him to stay? Make more empty declarations? He'd been drinking away his demons for years, or trying to. Why would this time be any different?

She pulled in a deep breath and tried to shake off the surge of sorrow. There was no time to wallow in such nonsense, she had a business to run. Her mind made up, she headed to her office, hoping to hide out a while until she could pull herself together.

"Miz Addie?" Abraham's deep voice came from behind her. "Is now a good time?"

"For what?" She winced at her sharp tone. Whatever the cause of her mood, it wasn't the poor man's fault. He'd been a loyal employee for many years, he deserved better.

"To talk." His brows raised in question. "You remember last night how I asked if I could talk to you 'bout something important? You said catch you in the mornin' 'fore it gets too busy."

She put a hand to her forehead, struggling to recall the conversation "Yes, of course. Come on in."

As they entered her office, she spied a letter atop her desk. Though it had only arrived a few days ago, she knew the contents by heart. Some lawyer in Cheyenne, represented Clancy Willowby the younger brother of her late husband Farley and claimed something about Clancy having loaned Farley the money to buy the social club all those years ago.

It was time for Addie to pay it back.

Adding insult to injury, he'd tacked on a nice chunk of interest, too, probably intended to make the amount out of her reach. If she didn't pay it by December twenty-fourth, she'd have to turn over ownership of the social club to Clancy.

The hell she would.

She snatched the letter up and stuffed it in the top drawer. Abraham stood in the doorway, looking hesitant. "Come in, come in," she urged, trying hard to keep the impatience from her voice.

He took a step forward. "Is it all right I close the door, Miz Addie?"

She gave an impatient wave. "Yes, yes. Come on now; we're burnin' daylight."

He strode toward the chairs in front of her desk, hesitating until she gestured for him to sit. "Land sakes, Abraham, you're a free man. You don't have to wait for me to give you permission to sit."

"Yes, Miz Addie." He sank into the chair, his large form seeming to overflow it.

She gazed at him sitting there, and a wave of tenderness assailed her. He was a big part of her success. Before he came along, brawls and drunkards were a regular occurrence at the social club. Now, he stood near the door of the club like a sentinel, the tall frame and bulging muscles a presence of their own. A quirk of a brow or a clearing of his throat and the patrons jumped to attention.

"What can I do for you, hon? You lookin' for a raise?"

He seemed uncertain what to do with his hands and he settled them on his thighs, clenching and unclenching his fists. "No, ma'am. But if you're offerin'…"

The edges of a smile teased her lips. "Course. An extra dollar a week, how's that sound?"

"Well, it'd help a lot, 'specially now. Now that I…" He flexed his fingers and rubbed a hand over his thigh.

She settled her arms on the desk. "Hon', you're just gonna have to spit it out."

"I come to ask your permission on marryin' Miss Emerald." He blanched. "I know I should'a done it years ago, but now her bein' in the family way an' all, I want to do right by her."

As the air left her lungs in a whoosh, she sat back in the chair. Pregnant?

Abraham's dark brown eyes remained intent on her. "You must know we been seein' each other a couple years now. I been after her to marry me a long time but she always sayin' no, she likes it here, she's happy." He leaned forward, his face creased with anxiety. "Please, Miz Addie, say somethin'."

She swallowed, trying to tide the panic rising in her chest. "Abraham, you know I'd never stand in the way of you marrying Emerald, especially with a little one on the way."

He rose to his feet, a big smile creasing his face. He reached for her hand, pumping it so hard her shoulder near came out of the socket. "Thank you, ma'am. Thank you, Miz Addie."

"You make that little gal happy now, you hear?" She said it as he all but ran from the room, footsteps pounding up the staircase, probably to find Em and tell her the good news.

She pulled open another desk drawer and caught sight of the bottle of amber liquid she'd confiscated from Russ this morning. She shook her head in disgust and moved it aside. Damn him for not being able to kick the stuff.

And while she was damning men, why not her long-dead husband? If there was a document around here, saying he owed his brother money, why had she never come across it?

She put her fingertips to her temples. Somewhere in the other room, Amethyst and Opal were practicing the songs they sang to entertain the men while they waited. With Christmas just a week away, they had chosen to add a few yule songs into their routine. The loud piano and repetition of *Deck the Halls* hit every nerve ending in her spine. One more *fa-la-la* might send her head exploding.

As the music ended, more voices carried in from the gathering room just outside her office. "Well, I think if we group the chairs in a circle in the dining room, it will work." Cornelia's voice carried to her from the other room. "We can have Abraham push the table aside for now."

"That ought'a work just fine," came the thick Irish brogue of her longtime cook, Aoife McCarthy. "I'll get the cookies goin' and make sure there's plenty of tea."

"Good idea, Auntie Eefie, and make sure we don't let them stay too long. Coyote and half the men in town think there's a storm coming, those cowboys will all be eager to get in one last visit." The gurgle of a baby and the pounding of small feet came. "In fact, I'll talk to Mother about closing down early, so none of them get stranded here tonight."

9

Addie frowned and hurried out the door. What was her daughter doin' here in the middle of the day?

Her grandson, Samuel Jr., toddled past and she reached for him. But instead, he ran to Aoife, who held out one of her famous sugar cookies. She scooped the tot up and kissed his cheek.

Jealousy gnawed at Addie's insides, but then Aoife had always been good with children.

Aoife saw her looking and beamed a smile. "And here's your *Mórai*, there she is." She jostled the tot and held him up as Addie reached her arms out to take the boy. She placed a kiss to his soft, pudgy cheek.

"What's this about movin' my table? And Liza Jane, Lord, in your condition you shouldn't be—"

Her daughter pulled herself up straight. "I am expecting, not dead. I cannot bear the thought of twiddling my thumbs and knitting booties for the next six months, waiting for this child to be born." She hurried across the room with all the grace a pregnant woman suffering from morning sickness could muster. "Here," she said, nodding as if she'd made up her mind. "Let's put the table here."

"For what?" Addie asked, pausing to nibble the cookie being held to her mouth by pudgy little fingers.

"The sewing circle," Cornelia snapped. "It's my turn to host. I asked you about it last week."

"I don't recall sayin' yes," Addie reminder her.

"Yes, well you said 'we'll see', Adelaide, so many times that I stopped asking." Cornelia huffed before turning away. "Aoife, I think this will do."

Anger shot down Addie's spine. Sewing circle? Here? That meant every busybody in town—most of whom were just dyin' to get a gander inside—would be under her roof. Lord only knew what gossip they'd be sharin' afterward. "Over my dead body."

She said it with such force the other women turned to stare at her.

"This is a place'a business," she said, emphatically, jostling her grandson who'd started to fuss. "Not some cozy little home for women to come socialize, drink tea, and gossip."

Cornelia's jaw dropped. "But Adelaide, they'll be here in—"

"I said *no*." The shrill sound echoed in the room.

Aoife tipped her head, frowning. The two had known each other, lived under the same roof for enough years that she could keep nothing from Eef.

An aching sensation began to build in the back of her throat. She kissed her grandson, handed him to his mother, and turned once again to escape to the sanctity of her office. She sat with her arms folded on her desk, head resting atop them, waiting for the emotional upheaval to pass. When the door opened, she didn't bother to look up. "If you've come to plead on your aunt's behalf, save your breath. This is a place for men to come and forget their troubles—"

"I think I know that after workin' here all these years," Aoife tut-tutted.

Addie raised her head. "Sorry. I figured you was that pushy daughter of mine."

The Irishwoman set a tray on the credenza near the desk and poured out a cup of tea. "You mind tellin' me what's the matter? You haven't been yourself for days, and you kicked that poor Mister Holt—"

Addie raised a hand. "I don't wanna talk about Russ. And I'm fine. Just havin' my lady time, that's all." She reached for the cup and took a sip. She didn't want to worry Aoife. Besides, she couldn't take a chance on someone overhearing. The entire house would know her situation in a matter of minutes. Before long, the whole town would know.

"All right, have it your way. When you're ready to talk, you know where to find me." Aoife walked toward the door, then stopped to look over her shoulder, pinning Addie with a knowing gaze. "But until then, keep in mind. I do the laundry around here, and I know who is on her monthly and who isn't."

****

Darkness came early this time of year. But Addie was relieved to see the sun finally set. One more day she'd gotten through without Clancy Willowby and his lawyer turning up on her doorstep.

The club was full, the men relaxed and happy, the chatter mostly about the snowstorm making its way across the territory. Newspapers and telegraphs to the sheriff said it would be a bad one. Opal played the piano while Pearl sang and told jokes and off-color stories to keep the men entertained while they waited their turn.

Addie paced back and forth, unable to relax. Russ would be busy with the animals at the ranch what with the storm coming. So why in hell did she jump every time the bell over the door rang, hoping it was him?

Lord but she loved that man, more than she'd care to admit. But until he decided to crawl outta that bottle and sober up for good, they were done. She'd spent too many years of her life trying to love him out of his pain, but he preferred the company of the ghosts that haunted his mind and that rotgut more than her.

When the bell rang again, her gaze moved toward the door. Her stomach dropped in disappointment when two men walked in, pausing to remove their hats and overcoats. Since neither of them was the tall, lanky cowboy with the shoulder length gray hair that she wanted to see, she turned away.

"We're here to see Mrs. Willowby."

Addie stopped short. There was an old-states-accent in their voices, not the lazy kinda way everyone talked around these parts. Her heart began to pound.

"You got an appointment?" Came Abraham's deep voice. "Miz Addie don't see no one without an appointment."

"We sent a letter telling her we would be paying a call."

Addie turned, her blood running cold at the sight of the stout, balding man and his tall, well-dressed companion. She hadn't seen Clancy Willowby since the day she'd married his brother, but he looked enough like Farley that she'd recognize him anywhere.

Abraham's dark gaze met hers. "That true, Miz Addie?"

For a split second she debated asking Abraham to show them out. Not to let them back in. But what good would it do, they'd just be back later, maybe with the sheriff. No, she needed to face this one head on.

Lord how she wished Russ were here. He'd know how to handle these two. But she'd learned a long time ago to rely on no one but herself. Men would only let her down. She drew herself up straight and walked toward them, her hand extended as though greeting long lost friends.

Damned if she'd let them see her sweat.

****

Long after the house had grown quiet, Addie sat in her office, staring at the grandfather clock. Everything she'd built, everything she'd sacrificed for—as good as gone.

That fancy lawyer, Elliott Charles, sure sounded convincing. He'd shown her papers signed in Farley's hand that said he'd borrowed the money to put down on the club and if he didn't pay it back in full in twenty years, ownership would transfer to Clancy.

She didn't wonder for a second why that ne'er do well Farley Willowby hadn't told her about the arrangement, she'd have skinned his sorry hide.

But now, all these years later, the chickens had come home to roost. If she couldn't prove them wrong, or find some document saying Farley paid it back, she'd lose her business.

Her girls would either be out on the street or forced to work in ways they hadn't done in years. Truth was, the whores at The Wylder County Social Club wasn't whores so much as companions. The men didn't know that, but some herbs mixed in their drinks gave them pleasant naps and very satisfying dreams. All the girls had to do afterward was tell them how good they were in the sack.

Deceptive? Yes.

Immoral? Maybe, at least according to Eliza Jane.

But it was how she kept her place clean, how she moved so many men through in a night. No sex meant no diseases. No diseases meant fewer headaches for her—and healthier men around town.

She pulled open her desk drawer, hating herself as she did so. The bottle was near empty. It'd been full when she'd taken it from Russ this morning. And it'd been full when Farley and his fancy pants lawyer had left.

The amber liquid glugged as it filled her teacup. She'd likely hate herself come morning—she already hated herself for being a hypocrite. She'd harped on Russ like an old nag about his drinking. Yet the first sign of trouble and here she sat doing the same damn thing.

Should she find him and apologize? They weren't married, after all, despite Russ proposing every other week. The cup came to her lips as if it had a mind of its own. She swallowed it all in one gulp, welcoming the mind-numbing warmth that spread through her.

No, Russ'd show up. Sooner or later, he'd show up.

Til then, she needed to talk to Clancy. Alone. Maybe she could get him to settle for less if that lawyer wasn't there talkin' out both sides of his mouth.

She rose, swaying a bit unsteadily on her feet. Wind rattled the windows outside, reminding her of the coming storm. For a moment she considered waking Abraham and having him accompany her. No, that wouldn't be right, that would only wake Em and get her all worried, then she'd tell the rest of the girls, who'd wake Aoife... Besides, she didn't want it to look like she was tryin' to intimidate Clancy by bringing her hired man along.

Her reticule was in the bottom desk drawer, so she grabbed it. She checked inside to see her trusty derringer. Russ had given it to her years ago and taught her how to shoot. Not that she could hit the side of a barn—'less she wasn't aiming for it.

Aww Russ.

Agony stabbed at the back of her mind at the memory, but she forced it aside. There would be time to examine her feelings later, when all this was dealt with.

She dropped the little gun into the drawer, no sense borrowing trouble.

She wrapped her favorite shawl around her, the one Sarah Taylor had embroidered when she first come to town. Another rattle at the window and she grabbed her cloak as well. Her favorite mother of pearl letter opener caught her eye and she tucked it into her cloak pocket. Just in case she needed it for protection.

After all, it was late, and decent women weren't out alone at this hour.

Well, nobody had ever accused Adelaide Willowby of bein' a decent woman.

Chapter Two

The blistering chill of high winds blew across Russ Holt as he fought to stay on his mount. Diablo shied in retribution due to the blinding snow. Proof of the expected blizzard.

He'd left town and found his way to the eastern pastures. Given the storm, the mares would need to be brought into the ranch. And he was late to the task, colder than hell and coming off the drunk that had gotten him kicked from the social club. Addie had tossed him out on his ear, and this time she meant it. He wasn't expecting quick forgiveness, but it might have been easier than this hell's half acre he rode through right now.

He urged the quarter horse to head off a group of horses that weren't happy with the conditions. That or he was doing no good with his intoxicated mind.

"Yahhha...ha..." He shouted above the winds, tossing up the coiled rope in his gloved hand to wave them onward. What a damn fine fix. Freezing to death while his body fought off the liquor and his mind battled over happenings with Addie.

God, he loved her and the comfort of being near her, even to talk. But now he'd done it. He'd shown up one too many times full of the damn devil's drink. Most often she'd put him to bed in one of the empty rooms at the social club and let him sleep it off, then scold him and send him on his way before morning.

This time she'd been quick to toss him right out, though he reckoned more than his drinking was weighing on her. She'd been a bit testier and distant the last few weeks, and he hadn't been able to put his finger on her reasons. Something was bothering her, and she wasn't talking. It looked like lady luck had called it quits on him for good.

"Son of a bitch..." He doubled Diablo back to turn a stubborn horse that trotted away from the rest. He caught her, and his horse cut her into the group once more.

His head pounded and his nerves frayed. But his hands trembled, and it wasn't the cold that caused him to sweat. He lifted a gloved hand to his mouth and clamped down on the middle finger, pulling his hand out of the mitt. He reached inside his heavy duster to pull the metal flask free and juggled to loosen the lid with frozen fingers.

A small sip would get him through, steady him enough to work. He sucked in a deep breath and tossed haste to the wind and gulped...twice.

The liquor went down with a warm, comforting burn that steadied him for an instant. He closed his eyes, letting it take effect.

"Hey, lay off the liquor, Uncle Russ." Astride his mount Jericho, Caleb was forced to yell to be heard over the wind. "We ain't got time for your slacking in this storm. Should've had these in by now."

He cursed under his breath. "Man can't even take a sip without all the shoutin'." He capped the lid, shoving it into his coat pocket, and pushed his hand back into the glove. His son—who still called him uncle—took off ahead and pulled the horses together and herded them toward the ranch as he followed.

An hour later the mares were secured as Cade Anson and Ed Cartwright brought in herds from the northern fields. Both hands had been on the ranch for years now. Such was life on a horse farm with mothers and foals inside the corral and others where they could fit or closer to the barn and large corral.

And now the whiskey had done its job. Maybe a little too well. The big barn blurred as he rode Diablo inside. He stood in the stirrup to dismount and put his feet to the ground. "Hell's fire coming down out there tonight. What say you boys?" His speech slurred as he turned. Caleb shoved him back, making him stagger.

"What the tarnation?" he sputtered, gaining his stance though he shouldn't be the least bit surprised.

"We been out in this for hours to save the herds, and you drag in here piss drunk once again." Caleb stepped even closer, his fists balled. "Can't run this ranch if I can't count on you and where are ya...on a drunk...when does it end, Uncle Russ. When?"

"Ain't drunk...just..." His speech slurred again, and he stopped. Hell, he was drunk and there was no sense lying. They all knew anyway.

"We lost two foals out there because we thought you were out pulling them in. But guessing you were too busy at your usual. Well, I'm done, Uncle Russ. If you can't pull your weight, it's time for you to go." Caleb threw his hands into the air with a growl but the other two said nothing in his defense.

And there it was again. Addie done with him and now his son, the two that somehow mattered most. It all came crashing down to send him through the big hole in the earth that had been waiting to swallow him up for years. He bent and lifted his hat from the dirt floor, snow falling from his duster. He placed it back on his head, looking at all of them and sobered by their reactions. He'd disappointed each of them over and over. But hurting Addie yet again and now Caleb…he turned and with some effort mounted up on Diablo. Without a word he raced back out into the cold of the storm, not looking back.

****

Russ sat alone at a table in the far corner of the Five Star Saloon, staring at the shot of rotgut before him. The small glass of bronze liquid sat idle as he contemplated what he'd become. Not what Addie thought of him, not what his son thought of him, but what he beheld of himself. He puffed on the skinny cigar between his fingers and blew out a cloud of smoke.

Across the saloon Sonny Cash dried and stacked clean glasses behind the long bar.

"A damn no good drunk," he whispered to himself.

The place was full, a few games of five card draw at tables on the other side of the room. Piano music spilled across the saloon, mingling with his thoughts, confusing him further.

He glanced at the drink again. One small glass at a time or the whole bottle…it mattered little…Addie was right. He was no longer the man he even thought himself to be. Hell, he wasn't the same man as clear back to Sarah. And he'd loved her with all his heart, the same heart that broke when she'd chosen his brother Rick.

He'd left Wylder out of necessity, letting his

brother raise the son that by rights belonged to him. But the shredding of his heart had come much later when he'd lost his second wife and daughter to a fire while out hunting. He hadn't been drinking then, not even a little—and look what had happened.

He wrapped his fingers around the small glass and with the other ground out the butt of the cigar. He'd buried his wife and later his brother, though nothing had come close to the pain of placing his small daughter in the ground. He pushed the glass aside once more, the bronze drink the one thing between him and the hurt that never ceased.

But Addie. Her touch brought a calm to the storms inside his heart and eased his mind. This time, he'd seen it in her precious blue eyes. He'd gone too far. Something lost, hidden behind disappointment if he were guessing. She was done, and he damn well knew it. The decision was now his to make...the bottle or Addie.

Dalton Payne kicked out a chair and sat, easing his cane and running a hand across his knee. "Some say a man finds peace in that drink...others not so much."

Russ glanced up at the famous gambler who'd returned home to Wylder some time back. The man always dressed in fine clothing and boots that carried a shine, at least when he was in town on some kind of business.

"Some don't know the ghosts of Christmas past."

Dalton nodded to the whiskey. "It takes a man who knows the woes to call another out."

He pulled in a heavy breath and eyed the younger man whose past drinking had cost him a knee in a bad play of poker years before. He let go of the small glass and leaned back into his chair. "What're you doing out in this storm?"

Sonny set a mug of Sarsaparilla before Dalton, who lifted his brows in relief of sorts and shrugged. "Brought the Doc's wife, Eliza, back home. Leona was feeling a bit poorly, but it seems to have passed." He smiled at his friend who seemed settled and happy in his newfound life.

"That's a good thing. You need to get on back to her then. Long time coming for you, Dalton, to have a family, a baby coming soon."

The gambler beamed a satisfied smile. "Never thought a family was in the plans for me, but now I've Leona and Gideon, though I imagine a baby to stir us all a bit."

"Keep everyone up at night." Russ nodded. He'd always thought well of Payne for his kindness to others, even taking in Gideon, a boy with no family. Some men were heroes and never even knew it and others...he glanced at the drink before him once more.

"Hell, I don't sleep anyway with this leg, but leastwise I'm still on the move." Dalton narrowed a hard gaze on him and then the small glass of liquor. "I've never asked ya before, Russ, but..." He hesitated but went on. "You want some ideas on that drink right there and how to kick it? I've been there."

He figured the man for a length of time. "Caleb put you up to that?"

The retired gambler shook his head. "Nope." He leaned up went on. "But I know that drink and what it does to a man when you let it win."

Dalton knew him as well as any and had never judged him for it, so why now? He said nothing.

"I'm proof it can be done, Russ, but there's not one thing easy about it." Dalton pulled the small shot of whiskey to the center of the table away from him. "Look at it again, real hard like."

Russ slid his gaze to the whiskey.

"Lesson one, every time you want it, and I know what that's like, you think about things real hard."

He glanced up at the gambler.

"Not a day goes by I don't still think about it. But I have my knee to remind me what it's taken from me." Dalton's voice dropped to a whisper. "And now with Leona, I am reminded of everything one sip can take from me if I fold my cards."

Russ looked at the whiskey again. "Guilty."

Dalton stood, grabbing his cane, and settling himself against it. "Is that drink right there worth folding on the things you love…Caleb and all those grand boys of yours…or say…Miss Addie…only you can decide. You let me know when you need help. You and I will take off to the woods and work on building a cabin."

Russ chuckled. "Build a cabin?"

"Hard work away from town with me in charge." Dalton smiled. "No drink found there. You get sober and you'll have something to offer the madam."

Russ squinted at how Dalton was so smart to things. "What're you hanging out with the quiltin' circle ladies these days?"

The gambler chuckled. "Be surprised what you can learn if you listen…"

Ezra Barlow bolted inside, covered in snow, and came to a halt. "Someone's been found dead by the hotel in the alley. Gutted with a knife."

Russ narrowed his gaze across the room as men gathered to hear more.

Dalton turned back toward him as he stood, leaning on his cane, the reason the gambler had given it all up, that and no real need for more money. "Some things never change."

Patrons of the saloon ran out into the streets while others echoed from inside.

"Who is it?"

"Who done it?"

Men hung over the saloon's double swinging doors, trying to catch a glimpse of the action outside. Hard winds sent snow blowing in all directions. By morning, the mud-covered streets of Wylder would be solid sheets of ice.

Russ walked up to stand beside Dalton, listening to the whispered chatter.

Sheriff Branch Wylder walked ahead of a group of men leading a small mule-drawn wagon. Inside lay the corpse of the man Ezra spoke about.

"They know who done it?" someone shouted again.

The questions kept coming. "Sheriff arrest anyone?"

"Heard some men tell the sheriff he'd been to the social club but left there shortly before." Ezra beamed with a hint of pride, watching from inside. The son of one of the best gossiping churchgoers in town, he was fond of being the first to share news, often found where he needn't be and wasn't to be trusted to keep any secrets. That apple hadn't fallen far from the tree.

In respect for the corpse, Dalton removed his hat and leaned closer. "Now what do you suspect happened here?"

Russ pulled on his heavy duster, settling his hat to his head. "Not sure. But the better question is where the hell's Addie?"

Chapter Three

Addie opened one eye—and slammed it shut as bright sunlight knifed into her lids.

Her head spun, her stomach threatened to erupt, and the hounds of hell had themselves a merry chase inside her brain.

Somewhere nearby, voices murmured in some vague discussion. She recognized Aoife's brogue. Then Ruby's sweet, low croon. Lord it must be breakfast time. She'd never been sick a day in her life, but she'd have to tell Eef she was under the weather today.

"I've come to bring Miss Adelaide her breakfast." Aoife's tone was pleasant, but Addie recognized the steel beneath. She wasn't taking no for an answer.

"I'm sorry, ma'am, I can't allow that." A man's voice permeated the fog inside her brain. A man in her room? Not likely. She sat up. Too abrupt. Her head spun as she looked around at the sparse little room, the hard, lumpy cot, and the bars across the door. Where in the hell...

"Miz Addie." Ruby's face lit up at the sight of her. "Oh my! You look a fright. How you feelin'?"

Spying a bucket some clear-headed soul left by the cot, Addie bent over just before her stomach emptied its contents.

"Let me tend to her," Aoife said. "Just let me in there for a few moments—"

"Sorry, Mrs. McCarthy. I can't do that." Branch Wylder's deep voice held no sympathy. "She's a murder suspect. She isn't allowed to see anyone."

"Murder?" Addie raised her head, wishing for a split second that she could just die and get it over with. "What in hell are you—"

Her stomach heaved again.

When she'd finished, Aoife passed a cloth through the bars so she could wipe her mouth. "Murder suspect or no, Adelaide Willowby has a reputation to uphold in this town," she tut-tutted. "I've brought that woman breakfast for the last twenty years, today won't be any different."

Addie slumped on the side of the dismal little cot, waiting for her stomach and head to stop trembling.

"Mrs. McCarthy—"

"Sheriff?" Ruby asked, "that your gun there on your hip?"

Addie glanced up to see Ruby, hands clasped behind her, swaying side to side almost childlike. "Can I hold it? I'll bet it's real big and powerful. Like you." Through her fuzzy brain, Addie saw Ruby bat her lashes and give a well-practiced pout.

The sheriff's face turned red. "Miss—" He tugged at his collar. "I'm going to have to ask you to leave now."

"Sure. I can come back later if you like." The red head gave a saucy wink and turned back to Addie. "I brung your face paint, Miss Addie. Let me fix your face for ya."

Ruby moved closer to the bars to begin the process of wiping Addie's face clean and applying more rouge. As she did so, Addie turned her attention to Aoife, who advanced on the sheriff like a coyote on the hunt. "Sheriff, have ya ever had one of my homemade biscuits? Light as an angel's wings, they are—here, try one with honey." The Irishwoman cornered the poor man, all but stuffing the breakfast treat into his mouth.

With Sheriff Wylder occupied, Addie wrapped her hands around the bars that confined her. "Ruby, what in thunder is goin' on? What's he talkin' about, callin' me a murder suspect?"

The girl looked over her shoulder, then leaned in closer. "Miss Addie, some fella was found dead. Some of the girls say they saw him at the social club the other night."

Low on patience, Addie shook her head, barely able to focus. Her head still thundered, her stomach wasn't sure it was done heavin', and her heart pounded like a runaway train. "Half the men in this town come to the Club, what's so special about that?"

"Mifffuvv Mc—" The sheriff, still chewing, turned his head as Aoife stalked him with another biscuit.

"Miz Addie," Ruby whispered. "They're sayin' his name was Willowby. Mister Clancy Willowby. D'you know him?"

Addie put her hands to her face, rubbing at the rouge Ruby had applied. "Yes. He's Farley's brother."

Ruby's brown eyes were as wide as saucers. "Well, what was yer dead husband's brother doin' here in Wylder?"

Addie waved a dismissive hand. "It don't matter none. I talked to him and—" She stopped. Strange how her mind was blank. She remembered leaving the social club, remembered the cold wind and snow starting up. And then…nothing. Why couldn't she recall anything else except wakin' up here?

"Miz Addie," Ruby's voice held an urgent tone that chilled her. "He was found stabbed through the heart. And it were yor'n letter opener that done the stickin'."

****

How had she gotten herself into such a mess?

Addie lay on the cot in the sparse jail cell, anxiety threatening to overwhelm her. How had this happened? She'd asked herself that a thousand times. And a thousand more times she'd willed herself to recall something—anything—of last night.

She'd been angry. Upset at Russ, worried about how she'd ever find someone to replace Emerald—let alone someone who could keep the secret about how they handled the men. If that wasn't bad enough, she was scared near to death about losing the social club.

Could she have killed a man? Did she have it in her? There were those who called her a hard-nosed businesswoman. Well, she sure hadn't gotten where she was by bein' nice all the time.

But…murder?

She didn't think she was capable of that, but if anyone deserved it, that rotten low-bellied swindler Clancy Willowby surely had. He'd been a liar and a cheat—every bit as slimy as Farley—back when she'd known him. He hadn't changed a bit.

She bristled, recalling the way he and his slick lawyer had come into the club that night, struttin' about like peacocks in their fancy suits, actin' like they owned the place. Grabbing and groping at the girls. She'd been angry as a hornet, but held her tongue, instead greeting them like she didn't have a care in the world.

She could remember all of that like it was five

minutes ago. But for the love of all that was holy why couldn't she recall what came afterward? She prided herself on her abilities to keep track of events—she knew every client and their preferences even if she hadn't seen them in months. Yet last night was a blur, as if she'd lost her mind.

She turned to face the wall, still fighting the panic rising within her. How could this have happened? Hadn't she been through enough? Oh, dammit why hadn't she agreed to marry Russ years ago and left all this business nonsense behind.

But I can't bear to watch him drink himself to death, and that's what would have happened.

When she'd realized the long dead, good for nothing husband Farley was nothin' more than a liar and a cheat who'd deceived her, it was the club that had kept her going. It wasn't the kind of business she'd dreamed of owning when Farley was filling her young, impressionable mind with stories of finding their fortune out west. But it was hers.

Who'd a thought Adelaide Appleby O'Hanlon Willowby would have a head for business? But it turned out she liked being in charge, liked the control that came from making her own decisions. While Farley had been content to gamble, glut, and rut at her like a pig in heat when it suited him, running the business was all hers. She'd managed the money, the men and grown it into the success it was now.

No one would take that from her.

Once Farley died, there was no one to answer to. No one to tell her what to do or bark orders at her. Being in charge suited her better than most. More than that, she'd relished in it. It gave her a purpose, and the more she put into it, the more satisfaction it gave back. Unlike a husband.

She was happier without a man. Til that tall, lanky cowboy walked through the door. A smile like the sin of the devil and a bottle of liquor in hand. Dark hair that fell to his shoulders and a sparkle in those deep brown eyes of his. She'd sized him up then held up a hand to let the bouncer know she'd handle it.

She smiled, recalling how she'd sidled up to him.

"Sorry, cowboy, I can't allow you to bring that bottle in here. You want liquor, you'll have to buy it from me."

He pushed the brim of his hat back and regarded her with a lazy grin she'd soon come to love. "That a fact?"

When she nodded, he uncorked the bottle, tipped it to his lips and drained the contents. He then turned to set it on the porch just outside the door.

"You ain't gonna be much good to any of my girls tonight after that," she'd teased.

"I don't expect it'll matter much." He fell into step behind her. At the time, Crystal and Amethyst were both available and he'd chosen Crystal. And paid for the entire night.

He was back the next week and the week after that, always a different girl, and always paid for the whole night. It struck Addie that he didn't have a "type." Most men had a preference for blonde, or brunette, short or tall, big bosoms or little ones. Not Russ Holt. She figured he must be a man with a powerful appetite.

Finally, one week when he showed up for his regular Saturday night, Aoife pulled her aside and said none of the girls wanted to take him.

"Why ever not? He ain't hurtin''em, is he?" she'd asked, half panicked that the charming cowboy who made her heart race had fooled her.

"No. He's just…well, the girls say he's… tiresome."

"But he's payin' for the entire night," Addie pointed out. "His money's as good as the next fella's."

Aoife had clasped her hands in front of her. "Adelaide, I hate to tell ya, but yer cowboy ain't…" Her cheeks pinkened. "Sowin' his oats. He's just… talking."

"Talkin'?" It wasn't the strangest thing Addie had ever heard, not by a long shot. They had men who liked to be scolded, slapped, tickled, and swaddled like babies.

A burst of anger rolled through her. "It ain't like those gals are in a position to be so fussy. I'd say a cowboy who wants to talk is a sight better than one who wants his pecker licked."

"Agreed," Aoife said, hands clasped in front of her in that pious way she did when she knew she was right. "But it seems to me the girls could make a lot more money if they could see more than one man in a night."

Addie dropped into her chair, dumbfounded. "Then charge him twice what he's payin'."

"Now that would hardly be fair after all this time," Aoife scolded.

"Then let him set in the kitchen with you, Eef, he's harmless."

"Now wait just a minute there. I loved my Paddy to the ends of God's green earth, but if I wanted another man underfoot or in my kitchen, I'd have married again." Aoife's hands went to her hips. "Bad enough I had to chase your Mr. Willowby out as often as I did."

A giggle bubbled past Addie's lips. "I can still see you chargin' after him with that rollin' pin, Eef."

The other woman nodded, her bright blue eyes twinkling. "Taught him to keep his hands to hi'self, it did."

Addie sighed. "All right then, what do you suggest I do with Russ Holt?"

Aoife tipped her head, studying her. He's handsome as the devil, that one, and his money's good as anyone else's. Perhaps he could spend time with you."

"Me?" Addie snorted. "Eef, I don't want another man around anymore'n you do."

"A good-looking man who just wants to talk?" Aoife shrugged. "I can think of worse ways for you to spend your evenings, Adelaide."

And with that the little Irish woman turned and left Addie to her thoughts.

Just as she was now.

Addie sat up on the cot and looked around the darkened jail cell. The sheriff had gone, the night deputy had yet to arrive, and she was on her own.

What a fine fix. And miss him as she might, Russ most likely didn't even know she was in jail, damn him anyway. He was probably on the ranch passed out, or in one of the saloons sucking down the rot gut that would take him to his grave. She was going to have to figure this out for herself, and she still couldn't remember one thing that happened to land here.

She'd stepped off the cot and began to pace the tiny cell when the ground rattled beneath her. From outside came a screech and crash as if Hell itself had

burst forth from the earth
What in the world?

Chapter Four

Darkness filled the sky as the high winds of a blizzard sent blinding snow across the town of Wylder. Several feet of snow already covered the ground.

Russ sucked in a deep breath and pulled his coat farther around him, cursing old man winter once and for all. It was colder than a damn well-digger's ass, but after hearing that the murdered man had been to visit the social club, he had best check on Addie and see what the hell she knew about it.

Regret nagged at him. He should have kept his hind end on the ranch. Well, Caleb would forgive him same as Addie in time. At least for now, anyway, his drunk was worn off.

He crossed the train tracks on foot, glancing at the line that led all the way to Cheyenne. Something was amiss, and it wasn't just the dead man. The afternoon train was overdue. Knee-deep snow hid the tracks leading out of town as far as the eye could see. At best it was the weather held the train up somewhere between Council Bluffs or Cheyenne.

He trudged ahead toward the social club and made it up the front steps, kicking away the piled-up snow that already covered the tracks of the latest customers.

He knocked at the heavy wooden door but let himself in as Abraham met him. The bouncer gave a slight bow, respectful as always. "Mr. Holt, you ain't

35

supposed to be here, you done heard Miz Addie."

Russ removed his hat and pulled off one glove at a time. "I know, but where is she? There's something important I need to ask her."

The freed man's face showed no expression. "Not sure I know, Mr. Holt. She done went out earlier and ain't returned."

"In this hell of a blizzard?" Russ narrowed a gaze on the man before him, a man who would protect Addie with his life if necessary. There was a fine line between lying and not telling what was known—and Abraham was doing a good job of the latter.

The younger man shook his head. "You know when Miz Addie get her mind to something ain't no stoppin' her."

He gave a nod of agreement. What the hell would that woman be up to on a night like this except…He turned and glanced out the window. "She out lookin' for me?"

"Don't know, sir. She awful mad at you. Told me not to let you back in either." Abraham dropped his gaze. "I need to ask you to go now, Mr. Holt. Be for the best."

Russ gave him a hard glare. Abe was an honest man and if Addie was here, he'd have said so. "All right then, but you tell her I'll be back come morning." He placed the hat back on his head and turned to go, though it did occur to him the social club was unusually quiet. Either the weather held things to a calm or most of the men had been given their tonics and drifted off to their sleep.

Abraham went to the door and opened it, waiting until Russ stepped closer. "Mr. Holt, might be best you let Miss Addie fume a spell longer."

He might have chuckled but a loud screech of metal and an explosion like black powder at the mines sounded and echoed like a thunderstorm.

"What the tarnation?"

****

Russ followed a group of men on horseback through the droves of snow piled shoulder high on the horses. He did his best in the shearing winds to steer Diablo in the tracks made by others to allow the horse to move faster. All around him, men made their way toward the blooms of black smoke in the distance.

Riders had come back into Wylder earlier with the news the incoming train from Cheyenne had derailed a few miles outside of town and collided with a snowbank. That explained the sounding crash that had echoed over the town of Wylder. A full moon held against the darkness, a line of smoke that billowed into the distant sky. Russ guessed the ice and snow from the blizzard had tossed the steam engine off its rails.

"Sweet merciful Jesus." Cade Anson pulled his horse to a stop alongside him. "Lord, have mercy."

"Ain't no mercy in this." Russ dismounted as a scurry of men continued searching the jumbled mess of overturned and remaining cars on and off the tracks.

Ed Cartwright rode toward them on their arrival. "The dead are being taken there to your right, and injured are being taken in sleds and wagons. Got a lot injured and still more trapped."

Across the way at one of the overturned cars, Caleb's hat bobbed in the wind. Word had traveled fast throughout Wylder, and help was coming in every form that could make it.

"Best get back out there." Ed dismounted and followed him and Cade ahead.

Russ plowed through the deep snow, stopping at the first overturned rail car he came to. He grabbed the side, bending to peek in the window—too dark. He glanced behind him, but the other men had found their way to help in various places. There was no order to this, find a car and hunt for people, listening for the wails and crying of the injured.

He kicked at the broken frame of a window and poked his head inside. It was dark, but a weary voice called.

"Here, please help us. Here!"

A shadow in the back of the car motioned to him. Russ wriggled his six-foot frame through the window, climbed past overturned seats and broken glass to get to what looked to be an elderly woman. He shoved piles of chairs out of the way and stood inside, trying to find his bearings in the darkness.

"We're here. Please," she called again.

"Coming, ma'am…" He moved toward the sound of her voice, finding it awkward to maneuver in the overturned car, there being little moonlight.

He found her, in the back of the car, pinned against the wall by a pair of seats trapping her there. "All right, gonna get you outta here."

"Please, I'm all right, but my husband. He isn't answering me any longer." She was an old woman, as best as he could see, her hair mussed, her clothing torn, and her teeth chattering.

He bent down where he could see the husband she worried after. He bit the tip of his glove to remove it and touched the man's neck. A faint bobbing of a pulse flittered there. "All right, ma'am, he's alive, but I've gotta get you out from behind these seats before I can get him out."

He stood again and glanced around the car and found a coat balled up on the floor. He shook it out as he moved back to her. "Cover yourself with this, I'll get you out of here, but it's a mite colder outside."

She took the coat and wrapped herself. "Thank you, but Henry, he hasn't moved, and I'm so afeared for him."

"Watch your head there, lean back, gonna try and move this." He placed the glove back on his hand and put a fist around the legs of the first sections of seats and pulled with all his might. It didn't budge. Holy hell.

He adjusted his position and gave it another try, leaning all his weight against it and this time, he gained a bit of movement. If he, had it in him, he would have cursed, but given the lady before him, he bit his tongue. He growled with renewed effort and the seat gave way, taking him to his knees.

He sat back up, chest heaving from the exertion and faced the woman. "Can you move?"

He took her hand and she tried and made it to standing though she turned back for her husband when he moaned.

"Henry, Henry…" She called, she then looked at him again. "I don't even know what happened, this train just rolled through the night and then out of nowhere it seemed I was flying out of my seat. Never heard so much noise."

"I'll get him, ma'am. You steady enough to walk to that window I come through?" He moved the second set of seating back from the man who lay on his side.

"All right, I'll get there, just help Henry. Oh, dear God." The woman went toward the window still talking to him.

He cleared more debris and patted the man's face. He didn't move. Well, this wasn't gonna be easy. He got a hold on one arm and pulled him, dead weight until he tugged half his body over a shoulder and then stood as erect as he could inside the car. Groaning with the man's weight he stepped in behind the woman.

The woman sobbed as they made it to the window. "Oh dear, Henry. I do hope he is all right."

Ed stuck his head through. "You in there, Holt?"

"Yeah, help the lady and get me someone in here, got an injured man, unconscious." Russ struggled to carry the old man all the way to the window.

"Here, madam, just hold my hand and bend through the window." Ed spoke as the woman sobbed and sniffled but followed his directions.

Russ settled to the floor of the car, which, as it turned out, was the side wall. He huffed a breath and glanced at the man as he laid him down, his upper body by the window. He turned and saw a woman lying face down. He touched her shoulder, but she didn't move. He turned her. She fell back and her wide-eyed stare found him. Young and pretty. But a hell of a bruise to the side of her face. What a damn shame. Dead.

He might have been on a drunk a while back but he sure in hell wasn't on one now. He placed a gloved hand over her eyes and closed them with a muttered curse.

"Shove him through, Holt." Ed leaned inside, though Henry still didn't respond any.

Russ caught Ed's gaze and helped push the man

farther out the window, where another man held a torch for light. "Got another one back here, let me check."

He grabbed the old man and pushed. Cade came along to help and soon the full of the man's body was handed off to others.

Russ turned back to the young woman. Strange she didn't seem to be bleeding from anywhere but there was no doubt about her demise. It had to be the bruising to her face and head. He smoothed her clothing and if he were a praying man—nah it was too late for her any way. He lifted her into his arms and placed her at the window, then watched as someone pulled her free.

He glanced around the car once more and moved through. "Anyone here, hey…anyone here?"

The empty car echoed with his deep voice, but nothing came. He turned and made his way back to the window intending to crawl back outside until a squeaking cry found him.

He turned and it came again. The soft weak cry of a baby if he didn't know better. He stilled to listen, and it took a moment, but another cry found him. He dug under the rubble, moving items away, a table, seating, a curtain with a large rod. And then he spotted the infant, swaddled in blankets and covered by half a seat cushion.

"Well, I'll be…" He adjusted his position and drew up the newborn, a tiny thing, no way to tell if it were a boy or girl. The baby gurgled, fixed eyes on him even in the darkness and stopped crying. How on earth had the child survived such? He spoke to the infant in a soft voice. "I got you…it's all right."

He supposed the baby belonged to the dead woman if he were guessing right, but there was no telling. No mercy to be found here for sure.

Cade stuck his head inside. "Russ, better get out of there. Next car's catching fire."

"Coming, got a baby here…give me a bit."

The infant in his hands was wet, soaked through and he lifted the swaddles and let them fall away. The baby shivered and kicked as he glanced around and rounded up the curtains and tossed the rod aside. He made an effort to wrap the baby tight. A girl. She sucked her fingers but didn't appear to be hurt. Cold and hungry at best. He tucked her inside his coat, holding her still with his left arm as he lay down and scooted through the window back out into the winds and blowing snow.

Cade was right. Smoke billowed from the next two cars as he stood again with the man's help.

"They're taking the dead to the right over there and injured are being loaded up in sled wagons and the small wagons that haven't mired, just ahead." Cade pointed. "Get the baby to some help."

He nodded, caught his breath, and trudged ahead. What a hell of a start for a little one. He trudged through the knee-deep piles, looking ahead where several wagons were pulling up, men and women helping where they could but the scene before him one of total chaos. Men on the far side were lighting cloth torches to give more light, still others were shoveling snow to the fires. And everywhere, people stumbling along calling for their loved ones. What the hell a mess this was. He had to get back out there.

He made his way across to the closest wagon.

"Got a baby here, little one, think she's all right." He shouted above the winds to the ladies in a wagon who had gathered up several children. "Can you take her?"

"Hand her to me." A woman held her arms out as he tugged the baby from inside his coat and handed her off. "Oh, lands. So small, this one." She hugged the infant and covered them both with a blanket and huddled the other children closer as the wagon pulled ahead for town.

Russ turned back to the derailed train where men worked in droves, others bringing wagons closer. He turned a full circle. Hell, this was not what he'd anticipated in traipsing around town trying to find Addie, who to his best guess was back at the social club by now.

"Uncle Russ." Caleb met him as he moved toward another car, his son out of breath. "They've enough men to continue the search, they need a few to get back to town and help set things up at the social club for the injured. Some are going there and some at the Wylder Hotel."

He shook his head squeezing his hands tighter as he couldn't feel them. "The social club?"

"Doc's gonna care for the injured there in the drawing room." Caleb shrugged. "At least those who need a lot of care, broken bones and the like."

"You going back?" he asked, glancing to where he'd tied off Diablo.

"No, they need me here, you go on, help with getting cots and beds from around town into the club for beds. Tables, too." Caleb shouted as he tromped back to the work ahead.

Russ gave him a nod, suspecting Caleb had volunteered him to get him out of the weather if nothing more. His son still thought him on a drunk. Nothing like a derailed train out on God's half acre of snow to cure that. But then, he had a know how about the order of things and could get work done when he set his mind to it. He turned to head for Diablo.

A man in a dark suit rode up on his mount, bundled in a fancy heavy coat and carrying a lit torch. "Sir, there?"

He lifted his gaze, squinting in the wind at the man he didn't know.

"Have you seen two men, should have been on the train, from New York?" the man asked in a huff. "Would've been dressed well, bankers...any sign of them?"

He gave the best answer he could. "A lot been taken to town, others dead, no sense of it all right now."

"Sir, these men, as I said, are bankers, headed to Wylder on business and we must find them." He circled his agitated horse.

Russ shook his head. "Look around you, a wreck like this don't pick sides." With that he turned and trudged on ahead toward his horse, leaving the jackass to his own.

Chapter Five

Addie tossed on the cot. Her stomach still felt off and her head had yet to cease pounding. Damn these foggy memories, if only she could remember... She closed her eyes. Maybe if she stayed absolutely still, something, some memory would come to her...

The tail of a yellow moon moved passed the window as Russ lay with his head in Addie's lap. She leaned against the headboard, embroidering a handkerchief. Normally, she'd be in her office going over the books this time of night but spending evenings with him meant taking things a bit easier.

He'd been lying here talking for a few hours now. She listened—mostly. He repeated himself a lot, so she didn't always hang on every word. Just enough of 'em.

They'd been at this for weeks now, at least the weeks he got all the boys on the ranch paid and a few golden eagles in his own pocket. He would spend a couple of evenings in town at the saloon then, and wind things down with her at the social club.

"You sure smell good, woman." That southern drawl out of Tennessee could melt a bar of gold. Maybe that was why she listened without much complaint.

She smiled but didn't speak. There wasn't nothing wrong with a man having his drink and a warm woman beside him too, but Addie had put her foot down on him talking to her girls. True he was paying for their time either way, but she wondered if he really preferred to chat and know a woman well before he found himself lying between her thighs—or if he couldn't rise to the occasion. She came out of her thoughts to find him staring up at her.

"I'm talking and that mind of yours is six miles away from here." He didn't change the tone of his voice. "You like all these things I tell ya or not?"

She flushed at getting caught gathering wool, especially since the wool she'd been gatherin' involved him. "I like 'em just fine, but seems to me you ramble off your drunk by chatting." She shook her head and drew the needle through the fabric once more. His initials were near done.

"Aw…well I ain't drunk…"

She raised her brows. "Not anymore you're not."

He lifted his head and pulled himself to lie beside her with his head on a freshly starched pillow Eef had left there. "I try to tell ya all the things I've seen and heard…like about the mountains in spring and pretty things just sitting right before us all." He closed his eyes and then opened one eye to peek at her.

She giggled. "I see you looking at me, Russell…and you know good and well I let you talk for hours in here to keep my girls working instead of being talked at."

"Well, I was paying them." He frowned up at her, busy brows raised. "Russell?"

"You were lingerin' is what you were doin'. That costs me money and time." She brought the thread to her mouth and bit through it. "And yes, Russell. It's a nice name, you should use it."

He stared up at her, a grin spreading over his face.

"So how come you never asked me to kiss you?"

She threaded the needle once more and twisted the string in a knot. Her insides were shakin' like an earthquake. "Kiss? Now, why would I do that?"

He sat up to lean against the brass headboard, narrowing a gaze on her. "I'm a good kisser ya know. Why don't you ask? Been in here hours at a time talking about the mountains and prairies and Indians and Mexico and Siberia for God's sake."

She ignored him and continued her work. He was handsome as sin, that much was true. But men only used kissin' as a means of getting elsewhere. She wasn't sure she was ready for that. She kind of liked her chaste life since Farley had passed.

He leaned up and settled his fingers around her wrist. "Well, no time like the present."

She pulled back, her breath hitching in her chest. "Russell Holt, what in thunder are you doing?"

He smiled as he eased his face closer to hers little by little. "I'm about to kiss you, Adelaide Willowby."

"You are?" Her breath halted, like she couldn't fill her lungs enough. And why'd her voice go all raspy like that?

"Yep. And you won't ever forget this one." He pinned her hand to the bed securing the needle stayed put and held her gaze for a long moment.

She didn't offer the slap he might deserve for bein' so fresh. She was too curious to find out what he was hiding under that big moustache. "Well, get on with it then."

He chuckled. "Call me Russell again."

She blinked, not sure she heard him. "Damn you, I'll call you Russell when…"

His lips met hers. Sweet. Warm. Just like him. A hint of cigars and whiskey.

Oh, she liked this. Maybe too much. This wouldn't do, her falling for his charms like this. She opened her lips to protest but her move allowed him the depth he desired. He teased and tasted until she gave a soft moan, she hadn't planned on givin'.

He eased a hand to her side, and she slid down in the bed, though he still held her wrist. She clutched the needle in her hand but didn't dare let go. He swept his tongue over hers. His hand fumbled, relieving her of the threaded point and setting it aside. Her hands found the way to his chest with a mind of their own, sliding the buttons on his shirt open.

He ended the kiss with a sigh and waited a second longer. Her entire being flushed with heat. He didn't hold her in suspense, he gave her more, adding the weight of his now shirtless body. She moaned and kissed him back, hanging on to him, wanting more in spite of herself. Oh, how long had it been since she'd ever been kissed like that? But the answer was clear…never.

He stopped. Withdrew his kiss except for one more nip at her lips as if he couldn't contain himself. "Told you I know how to kiss." With that he got off her and the bed and found his shirt pulling one sleeve on at a time.

She sat up, tucking back tendrils of hair that had come undone. "Russ…Russell where are you…going?"

He pulled a suspender over one shoulder and hopped into a boot at a time not bothering to button his shirt.

"What on earth…" she demanded, anger roiling

inside at his teasing her this way.

He leaned over and kissed her cheek. "Don't worry, Miss Addie, with that beautiful face of yours, I'll be back with more stories soon enough."

He headed to the door grabbing the knob. He opened it and turned just as she hauled a pillow his direction. He pulled the door closed with a chuckle as she hurled a string of profanity at him. Damn the man for leaving her wanting more.

Like she was now. She turned on the cot, cursing the darkness that surrounded her in the jail cell. The evening deputy hadn't shown up yet, and the night stretched on. She could tell from the commotion in town something bad had happened, but no one had come to check on her. Alone and forgotten. Not even Russ cared to stop by and see how she was faring— even though she had run him off.

Tears threatened but she refused to give in to them. Instead, she turned and fell back into a fitful sleep.

****

Moonlight illuminated the snow as Russ made his way toward the social club. Chaos was the word that came to mind as he took in the sights around him. Wagonloads full of wounded—and worse. Gus Wright, the town undertaker, had a full wagonload, too.

He pulled his hat off out of respect as the telltale black wagon went past. Poor damn folks. Never knew what hit 'em. What a thing to happen so close to Christmas. But he had worries other than the damn train. He needed to set eyes on Addie's face, know she was all right, hear her soothing voice. Didn't matter if she flew at him like a wet hornet first, he needed to see her. Especially since he'd never gotten to the bottom of the story the dead guy had been at the social club.

Outside Addie's place, several of the women from town were directing things. With the men all helping to unload the wagons, it left the women to do what they did best. Cornelia Appleby, Addie's sister, and Eliza Sullivan, Addie's daughter, were in the thick of things, telling folks where to take the wounded based on the severity of their injuries. Strange none of 'em even noticed him and that wasn't the case most often.

He climbed the steps to the front porch, stomping the snow from his boots before opening the door. No one greeted him, which was odd. But more unusual was the activity—people rushing around, women carrying basins of water, trays of food, and armfuls of linen strips he assumed for bandaging wounds.

Any other time, this drawing room would be filled with men waiting for the girl of their choice, and a drink that made them forget their troubles. Addie and the gals would play the piano and sing or tell stories to keep the men entertained. Now the piano and chairs had been pushed to the far corners of the room, something he'd never seen in all these years.

A cold blast of air from the door opening hit him, followed by a woman's voice. "Don't just stand there gawking, Mr. Holt, figure out what needs to be done and get to it."

He recognized the nasal northeast tone of Addie's older sister and cast her a glance over his shoulder. "I'm looking for Adelaide."

Cornelia waved a dismissive hand. "Mercy, who has the time to tell *that* story?" She didn't give him a chance to ask anything else, but pushed past him, calling orders to some of the other women. Well, some damn things never changed.

Across the room, Doc Sullivan had a patient lying on the dark wood table from the dining room. His sleeves were rolled up, his shirt stained with blood as he pulled sutures through an arm again and again.

Abraham's bulk had been put into use by the women. He was on the stairs, lugging a mattress to the first floor, while Em stood behind him, arms laden with blankets and pillows.

Cooing and laughing drew his attention to the center of the room, where Amethyst, Pearl, and Opal were fussing over the baby he'd found earlier. Someone had fashioned a makeshift bottle, and the infant was getting a full belly. Well, at least the poor little thing was warm and dry now.

He was about to move on to search for Addie when it struck him. Most often if there was a baby around, Aoife was front and center. Every mama in town who had ever had a colicky baby had called on her at one time or another. The woman had a gift with babies and couldn't get enough of them. Yet she wasn't anywhere to be seen.

The kitchen door swung open as someone came out and before it could close, he caught a glimpse of the gray-haired Irishwoman inside near the back door. Dressed in her heavy winter cloak and packing a basket of some sort. Something wasn't right. He was damn well about to get to the bottom of it. Cornelia acting stranger than usual; Aoife packing to head out into a storm? Addie nowhere to be seen, and this was the kind of situation she'd be right in the thick of. Something had gone very wrong.

He pushed open the kitchen door as Aoife was

about to slip out the back door.

He raised his voice, stopping the woman in her tracks. "What in hell's goin' on?"

She whirled, hand on her heart. "Russ Holt, you're a sight for sore eyes but ya nearly scared me to death."

"Where in the damn hell is Addie, and where the hell are you going on a night like this?" He walked past her and placed a palm to the closed door, blocking her way. He wasn't waiting another minute to find out what was going on.

The door banged open and Amethyst came in, rolling her eyes with a huff. "I'm going with you, Eef. I can't take that miserable woman another second."

"Which miserable woman are we speakin' about?" Aoife asked, rolling her eyes. "Half the gossip lovin' pea hens in Wylder are out there."

"Cornelia," Amethyst sulked, arms folded across her chest. "Oh hi, Russ."

Enough was damn enough, Russ folded his arms, standing against the door. "Ladies, I want answers and I want them now. Starting with where's Adelaide?"

Amethyst exchanged glances with Aoife, who shrugged and shook her head. "He doesn't know?"

A chill ran down Russ' backbone. "Know what?"

"All right. But you'll want to have a seat." The Irishwoman nodded at the table where a few chairs remained. "Amethyst, go round up the other girls—just make sure Cornelia doesn't see you."

A short time later Russ sat in stunned silence while Aoife and the girls told him everything. Aoife bringing Addie her usual cup of warm milk with nutmeg and honey at bedtime and finding her gone. Aoife and the girls heading out to try to find her before the storm could hit.

"We finally found her," Aoife said, clutching a hanky to her damp face. "She was barely conscious, murmuring nonsense about Farley. And…" Her voice broke. "She was covered in blood. At first, I thought she was hurt, but when we got her home and undressed her, there wasn't a mark on her." Tears filled her eyes. "There's only one reason I can think she'd have someone else's blood on her."

Addie a murderer? Not the woman he knew. She was tough as nails but when it came right down to it, she wouldn't hurt a fly. Unless they were hurting someone she loved, and even then, she'd find a way around all out murder. "Where are her clothes now?"

Amethyst and Ruby exchanged hesitant looks.

Ruby cleared her throat. "We burned 'em. Eef and us girls."

Russ sat back in the chair. If ever he had need of a drink, this was it. But it was more important than ever to keep his wits sharp.

"Tell' I'm about the letter, Eef." This from Pearl, who stood guard at the door.

"Letter?" Russ angled a glance at the woman he'd known every bit as long as he'd known Addie. More than once he and Eef had tied one on at this very table. Her and her damn Irish whisky.

"I burned that, too." Aoife twisted a hanky in her work-worn hands. "If the sheriff ever got hold of that…"

"What'd it say?" Russ studied the woman's face. He had no doubt Aoife would do anything to protect Addie, but she'd never lie to him.

The ladies at the table exchanged worried glances.

"It's probably best I don't tell ya," Aoife said with a hard shake of her head. "I don't want to worry ya, and that way if the sheriff comes 'round...Well he can't ask ya 'bout what ya don't know."

Russ' fist hit the table with a loud bang, and the room went silent.

Opal, quiet until now, jumped like a scared rabbit. "It was from some lawyer in Cheyenne. He said Miss Addie don't own the social club no more."

"No, he said she won't if she don't pay him by Christmas Eve," Amethyst clarified.

"He said Mister Farley borrowed a lot of money from his brother to buy the social club," Emerald spoke up for the first time.

Ruby glanced at the other ladies before speaking. "And he said if Miss Addie don't pay up, Mister Clancy will be the new owner and that would mean he owns all of us, too."

"Cep' Clancy is dead now." Pearl, still standing post at the door, shrugged.

Russ' mind swam with the information as the girls and Eef began talking over one another. No wonder Addie had been distracted of late. And damn the woman, it was just like her not to ask for help when she needed it, no matter how dire the situation. Always thinking she could handle things on her own. Well, as near as he could tell, she was in a fine mess of things now.

"So, there she sits. All alone while everyone in town is here." Aoife shook her head. "A train derailment, of all things to come about. I'm off to sit with her for the night, to keep her company and bring her warm milk and somethin' to eat. The sheriff didn't want to let me, but I told him a thing or two as well. He won't be keeping me from tending Addie as always I have."

"You were right to burn that letter, Eef." He pushed back the chair, shrugged on his coat, and strode toward the door. "Well, what are we a waitin' on?"

Chapter Six

Icy snow crunched under Russ' boots as he kept a
hand on Aoife's arm to steady her. The trek from the
social club across town toward the jail was dicey with
the blizzard still blowing. What were these ladies
thinking, planning to head out to the jail all alone?

Amethyst clung to his other arm as they trudged
along. Sometimes he wasn't sure who was holding up
whom.

Pellets of wet snow whirled around them, making
visibility limited and movement slow. The town was
busy what with the train derailment. People braved the
storm, bundled against the weather, trotting across
streets, and leaning into the wind. Many had expected
relatives to arrive for the holidays and were heading
from place to place, looking for information on loved
ones.

Men on horseback carried torches, lighting a path
to the outskirts of town where the demolished train lay
in heaps of tortured metal.

What a hell of a few days. How long had it all
been? Eef slipped, tugging at his arm, but righted
herself. Even over the wind he heard her muttered
cursing in her native Gaelic. If it hadn't been for the
distraction of Addie's situation he might have chuckled.
He pulled them all ahead until they reached the sheriff's
office porch piled with enough snow to keep it from

being much of a porch at all. A gust of wind buffeted snow at them, stinging his face. The ladies bent their heads as it pummeled them, as if it was trying to knock them off their feet.

Damn. He'd expected the blizzard to let up long before now, but it showed no signs of slowing.

Light from inside the jail glowed at the window but...hell's tarnation. Addie in jail. Given the story he'd been told, something smelled of a rat. He wanted to see her first—before he made a decision on how to proceed—even though there was no guarantee she wanted to see him.

He helped Amethyst to the door. She struggled to push it open, then held it for him and Aoife. He used both hands to assist Eef inside then followed her into the heavy warmth of the sheriff's office. He fought against the wind to shove the door closed, gulping a breath to recover from the brief fight. Hell, he was too old for this shit, though he reckoned his work in the cold was no closer to being done. He still had to face Addie and figure out what the hell was going on.

He turned and his gaze locked with Addie's through the bars of the cell.

"If it isn't colder than the devil's heart." Eef moved to the small wood stove in the corner, muttering the injustices of the weather.

Amethyst squeezed a bag of clothing to Addie through the bars along with a blanket and pillow she'd brought. "It's the things you asked about and some sandwiches the girls made." She brushed tears from her cheeks. "Oh, Miss Addie, you shouldn't be here. It's so cold."

Addie said nothing but watched him as he removed

his hat. They'd never needed words, but he could damn well read her thoughts loud and clear. He'd showed but was too damn late.

"Russell, you shouldn't be here." She spoke first but the sight of her holding onto the bars from the other side sent his thoughts veering right off their hinges.

Eef turned, lifted a log from the pile before turning to face her. "Adelaide, we'll be needin' his help, no?"

She shook her head. "You can tell Russell I can handle things on my own and will not be requirin' his help."

Amethyst darted a glance at both before edging away to help Aoife with the firewood.

Russ stepped up to the bars. "You can be angry at me later, right now I need to know what the hell happened out there and why you're in here?"

He glanced behind him at the other women, grateful there was no sign of Branch Wylder at the door, but supposed with the train crash, the lawman was pretty busy right now. He leaned in close. "Just say the word and I'll have you outta here. We can make our way to Mexico or Siberia…wherever you like."

Addie looked past him to address the other ladies. "You can tell Russell I won't be heading to Mexico or Siberia. One's too hot; the other's too cold." She folded her arms and turned her back. "Although, it's nice to see he's sober for a change."

He might have chuckled at her sticking to her anger, just as he'd expected. But this was too serious. "Too cold to be on a drunk." He shook his head and waited wanting answers. "Will you just tell me what in the hell happened? There's no time to play around here, Addie, once the tracks are clear the circuit judge will like to show up."

She looked over her shoulder, her face pale. "That's just it...I...can't remember a thing."

"Start from where you do remember...how about the letter?" He didn't have time for games. As soon as the train happenings were all ironed out and the snow cleared, she'd be facing a noose.

She jerked a guarded glance at her friend, grabbing the bars once more. "Eef...you told him?"

Aoife walked over in a rustle of skirts. "Addie, we can't do this alone. Ye know that, and we've no way to prove a thing even if you are rememberin'."

Addie let out a heavy sigh and looked at him again. "The letter came a few weeks back. The next thing I know, Clancy Willowby and some fancy dressed clod from back East walk through the door. Seems if I don't pay up, they are taking my place."

"How's that?" He folded his arms angling a hard gaze on her, things dawning closer to the edge of his mind from long ago. "Back up a ways. *Clancy* Willowby? Farley's brother?"

"Yes, surely you haven't forgotten the slimy leech. Only he's dead and I have no memory of it at all." Her voice climbed an octave with each word. "They say it's my letter opener that was found in him. The silver one with the mother of pearl and my initials. But how could I do something like that and not remember anything of it?"

Nope, he hadn't forgotten either of the Willowbys, though he'd never met either up close and personal like. "Yeah, I remember you said he stirred it up no matter where he was, but how would he have rights to the club?"

Aoife stepped toward them, holding out the cup of milk she'd warmed on the stove. "Addie, you must tell him everything. We cannot do this alone. You could hang. I don't wanna fight that with my own fists, but I will, and you know it." The Irishwoman's voice broke, this whole thing was taking a toll on them all.

Russ laid a hand on her shoulder as she dabbed at her eyes. Amethyst hurried over to wrap an arm about her and lead her away. "The place needs some cheerin' up. That's all, it's near Christmas anyway, Eef, it should look like it in here, too."

Addie's gaze was tormented as she stared after them. When she noticed him watching her, she tossed up her hands and stepped away from the bars. "Farley made lots a bad deals back then and he'd made one with Clancy…borrowed money to purchase the social club. But I own this club. I built it around them both, took every penny I had, too."

"All right, all right. What does Branch have on you?" He glanced at the door again. They shouldn't be here without permission. It could be only a matter of time before the sheriff, or his idiot of a deputy returned.

"Well, there's the letter opener. But like I said, I got the letter from the lawyer. And then last night Clancy and that lawyer barged in, giving me an ultimatum. I've no legal papers to prove the club is mine, but I started thinking it might be best if I just paid him to go away." She paced across the cell. "I got a little bit saved, so I went to the hotel to see Clancy— you know, away from that lawyer fella." She reached the other side of the enclosure and turned, her face alight with recollection. "I remember that he laughed and said he would rather take the club and I…I told him…them…"

"Them?" He pulled his coat off, the heat inside the jail now too much.

"That partner of his, Elliott Charles had come up by this point and was shaking his head." She stopped pacing. "He said there would be no deals and they would be assuming the club. "So, I…left them there and went back outside in the storm…I think Clancy followed."

She frowned, narrowing her gaze as she sought to recall. "It's…not clear…I was arguing with Clancy…and as I turned to go, he grabbed my arm, and I dropped my bag and bent to pick up my things…then nothing. Try as I may, I can't remember anything more." She returned to the bars, wrapping her hands around them. "Russell, why can't I remember?"

Russ rocked back on his heels. "Who's the other man? This Charles person?"

"I don't know him. Seems Clancy called him a business partner. A lawyer from Cheyenne." She squeezed the bars, her knuckles turning white from the force. "Much as I'd have liked to, I know I didn't kill Clancy. I couldn't."

"Adelaide, we know you wouldn't do such a thing," Eef said from across the room. "I've burned the letter, no one will know anything of it."

Russ frowned, stroking his moustache. "Charles, he got dark hair, wearing a suit with a top hat in gray?"

Addie nodded. "Yes, I…think so."

"He's out at the train derailment, hunting bankers from New York or somewhere." He wished there were no bars between them so he could take her in his arms. Wishing a lot of damn things. "Don't know what he might've found or not, but I'll head out that way and see about some answers." It would be a start.

"I assume he's Clancy's lawyer...I don't know. The letter called him a business partner and investor. But now with Clancy dead..." Addie met his gaze and for a moment he thought she might weep, but nope, not his Addie. "What are you gonna do?"

Russ put one of his hands over hers, surprised she didn't draw hers away. "Don't you worry. But you have to keep things quiet."

She pulled in a sharp breath, and he was pretty sure he heard her voice crack. "What're you going to do?"

He gave her a wink. "Gonna hunt out the fox in the hen house for starters."

The door scraped open and Branch Wylder stepped through, shucking his heavy, wet coat and hat. He drew up short when he spied them. "Hey, you all can't be here. Russ, you gotta get these women out and you shouldn't be here neither."

His new deputy, Ferguson, not the brightest of lawmen when it came down to it, tromped in behind him, his mouth dropping open. The much shorter, chubby man waved his hands toward the door. "You folks heard the sheriff. Move out."

Aoife rose from the chair. "I've already told you I'll be a bringing Ms. Addie her milk and biscuits each evening and her breakfast each morning."

"You gotta go, Russ, the ladies, too," Branch scolded. "She's a prisoner, like it or not." Then, he raised his voice. "Hey, what are you doing there?"

Across the room Amethyst tied red ribbons to each of the cell bars that contained Addie. "I am decorating things for Christmas since you won't allow her to wait at the social club."

She dropped a ribbon and bent to retrieve it, her plentiful assets straining at her bodice. She straightened, smiled like a cat with a fresh bowl of cream, and sauntered closer. "Surely you don't mind a few decorations, Sheriff?" she purred, running a hand over his chest.

Branch wasn't buying it, nor her flirting. He stepped back, ignoring Amethyst's pout. "Fine. You can decorate the cell. Now, I've got to ask you folks to go. We got too much going on with that train derailing. I'll have to lock the jail if you can't stay out of here."

Ferguson ushered them toward the door and cracked it open waiting on them to go, tapping a boot on the floor. "Come on, folks, Sheriff said to go."

Amethyst sashayed back to the bars, ignoring him as she tied the last few bows.

Russ placed his hat back on his head. "Got every extra bed found in the social club and saloon and the hotels are full...what more you got?"

"The social club?" Addie choked. "Oh, dear Lord."

"Identifying and placing those dead in the outer shack at the livery. If the storm didn't cripple us to the outside. As soon as this storm lets up, we gotta get the debris cleared and repair the track so the next train can make it in with relief supplies. I saw you out helping with the rest, Russ, but you can't come back here. Addie is allowed to see a lawyer and that's all." The younger man leaned closer. "You gotta keep these girls and Mrs. McCarthy outta here."

Had it not been for Addie's situation he might have been amused at the young, new sheriff, frazzled at the likes of Amethyst's flirting and Eef's stubborn insistence and no doubt overwhelmed with what was happening in town. Though he was a married man now, his ears still held a hint of pink from his encounter with both females.

"Come on, ladies. I'll get ya both back." Russ turned to face Addie. "I'll be checking on things."

She nodded, then beckoned the dark-haired girl closer. "Am...get Eef back home and see that she rests."

"I've no need of rest if ya aren't allowed the same," the older woman protested.

"Eef, you ain't had much sleep, if I know you. If you're gonna bring my breakfast, come morning, you need to get some shut eye." Addie reached a hand through the bars, touching her friend's hand. "I'm fine. Really."

Amethyst choked back a sob but tugged at Aoife's arm. "Come on. We need to get back and help with that baby 'fore Cornelia finds out we're gone."

"Baby?" Addie echoed. "What baby?"

Amethyst looked over her shoulder as she shrugged into her cloak. "A baby. And a group of nuns from the train. The nuns are helping care for the injured and helping Doc Coyote and feeding everyone."

"Nuns?" Addie yelped. "In the social club?"

"I'll tell ya all about it over breakfast," Aoife promised as she waited at the door for Amethyst.

Russ held back, ignoring Branch and his counterpart, who still waited at the door. He stepped closer to Addie and reached through the bars to brush a palm across her cheek. She grabbed his hand for a split second, surprising him.

At the door, Amethyst stepped up to the deputy and

planted a lingering kiss on his mouth. "See you soon, Fergie?"

The young lawman turned beet red and took a step back, grinning. He caught his boss' glare, put his head down and headed for his desk.

Russ exited to face the weather once more with the ladies. "That a friend of yours?" he asked when they were a safe distance from the sheriff's office.

"Not really," Amethyst giggled. "But it got me close enough to get this." She dangled a key, a look of triumph on her face. "Now we can visit Miss Addie whenever we want."

Chapter Seven

The nasal whine of the deputy's snoring kept Addie from sleeping. The young man had his feet up on his desk, his hat pulled low over his eyes. She couldn't blame him, what with all the fuss in town over the train derailment, he had to be exhausted. Probably wished he was sleeping in his own bed.

Well, he wasn't the only one who wanted to be home. Having her own pillow and blankets helped make it a little more comfortable and one of the girls had thoughtfully hidden a pouch of Aoife's sugar cookies in the bundle. But there was nothing lonelier than being wide awake when the whole world was asleep. Not even dawn was showing its face yet. Neither had Russell Holt. She hoped he was good to his word and would start looking into what happened instead of the bottom of a bottle in the Five Star saloon.

Restless, she paced the small cell, too worked up to sleep. Now she knew what penned animals felt. She spent way too much time walking the floor in here, it was never in her nature to sit still.

Hopelessness and despair threatened to overwhelm her at the thought of the tracks being cleared and the sheriff calling in the circuit judge. She put a hand to her throat, rubbing absentmindedly.

An ache began at the back of her eyes as she recalled Russ' offer to take her out of here. He'd never allow her to hang. For a moment, she indulged herself in the fantasy of her and him running off and starting over somewhere no one knew them.

Her heart plummeted. Away from their families, their children and grandchildren. He and Caleb were only just finding their way now that Russ had told him he was his true father. She couldn't ask him to leave behind a relationship he'd waited years to have with his son. And she and Eliza Jane were still trying to establish a mother and daughter bond after years of being estranged.

But he'd offered. Maybe in his own way he did love her. She'd spent years feeling cheated for losing her first husband so soon, and for the mistake she'd made in choosing Farley. Maybe with Russ she'd finally found the love she'd longed for.

Except for that damn bottle.

Frustration threatened to overwhelm her as she made her way to the other side of the cell. Lord, she wanted to curl into a little ball and sob her eyes out at the injustice of it all.

Had she killed a man? Wouldn't she remember if she had? She wasn't the sort of person who went about town killing folks, so something like that was like to stick in her mind, wouldn't it?

She ended up back at the cot and dropped down. She'd never liked feeling weak and had never been one to give in to the sensation. Even back in the early days with Farley when it had become clear he'd lied to her about pretty much everything and gotten her to leave her daughter behind, she'd never cried. No, she just put her head down and worked that much harder. Work had always been her salvation.

Until now.

She pulled up her feet to tuck herself into a ball and grabbed hold of one of the pillows, comforted to find it still smelled faintly of Russ. With the rhythmic whistling of Deputy Ferguson's snoring filling her ears, and the scent of Russ in her senses, she drifted into a fitful sleep out of sheer exhaustion.

The curtains fluttered around a window left open to catch a warm autumn breeze. Addie lay in Russ' arms, her body thrumming from his kisses and caresses. He had been spending time with her for months now, and though they kissed and touched, so far, he'd made no attempt to try anything more.

She knew about men who simply liked the anticipation, the hunt, the will she give in or won't she. She sure'n hell hoped he wasn't one of those.

Her relationship with Farley had been completely unsatisfying, causing her to wonder if her passionate relationship with John, her first husband, had simply been the exuberance of youth, or some rare good fortune. Sadly, just as they'd gotten past groping and fumbling through the act and learning how to please each other, he was gone. She'd never felt passion like that again until now.

She wasn't sure she could bear the disappointment if all these feelings Russ had stirred in her turned out to be for nothing.

His arm tightened around her. "You're thinking again, Adelaide. That's never a good thing."

The moans and cries of one of the girls carried to her through the walls, followed by the bang of a headboard hitting the wall multiple times. Just another Saturday night here at the social club.

"Someone is making one of your girls very happy," Russ murmured with a chuckle.

Addie laughed. "Or not. They're good actresses, you know. That sounds like Amethyst, she likes to put on a show."

Russ rolled to his side, propping his head up on his hand. "So is that what you were thinking 'bout?"

Addie dropped her gaze, feeling shy for the first time in decades. "Well I was kinda wonderin' why you never want to go any farther than touchin' and kissin'."

A slow grin turned up the corners of his thick moustache and his eyes crinkled in amusement. A look she had come to love in all these months. "Addie. I ain't some young buck in a hurry to sow his oats. I figure I can wait until you're ready." He tapped the end of her nose. "And if you're not plannin' to be ready any time soon, that's okay with me."

A rush of emotion poured over her. Was he sincere? A man who truly wanted to spend time with her, not use her for his pleasure and move on?

She took his free hand and pressed it tight to her bosom. "I've been ready for a long time, Russ, I was just waitin' on you."

His gaze darkened and she tugged down her bodice until one breast popped free. There was no need for words as he closed the slight distance between them, his hand covering her breast. His moan of pleasure echoed in her ears as he pulled her close, his mouth covering hers.

He gripped her hand in his, pulling it above her head as he settled between her thighs. He bent a head to feast at her breasts one to the other until she gave a soft moan.

He continued to tease and taste her, leisurely drawing hard on her nipple until she dug her fingers into his shoulder. "Russ, please."

Patience was never her strength, but he liked to take things slow.

"Not yet," he whispered. "Not gonna rush…open your legs, Addie…" He eased down her body and kissed her belly.

She moved back in the bedding, her thighs falling open.

He gave a growl and bent his head, kissing the place she wanted him most and beginning a slow, searing suck that made her writhe in pleasure. She moved against him as he scorched the tiny pearl time and again with his tongue and lips. When she was near mindless from pleasure, pressed his fingers just inside her opening and massaged.

She cried out, more than once, trying to buck against him though he held her, lapping the pearl, and working his fingers until the waves of pleasure stopped.

He crawled back up her body. "Damn beautiful Addie."

Her face had to be six shades of red. She ran a brothel, she knew the most intimate details about half the men in this town, knew all the bizarre and just plain strange things people did together in the bedroom.

But she had never been loved like that.

He lay beside her and kissed her shoulder, tasting her skin as his hands rubbed across her breast.

She gained her breath. "Russ…"

He smiled and brushed the hair back from her brow. And then moved to fill her slow and sure.

His groan matched her soft sigh as he began the

slow rocking. He wasn't in a hurry to meet his own desires. He seemed intent on loving her completely, every inch of her.

And where had he learned these things? No one had ever spoken of this kind of love. The kind where two kindred spirits became one.

She ran her hands along his shoulders, intrigued by the muscles there, still firm and sculpted as any younger man. She let her legs fall farther open, wanting to take all he could give her. And so began the dance of give and take. The dance against each other for the sweet release.

He drove harder and faster, no words needed between them as he lifted her knees to his sides. His hips pressed again and again as he nipped her breasts and then took her mouth. His kiss was of passion, his tongue teasing her own. She placed her hands to his shoulders and ran her fingers into his long gray hair.

"Open your eyes, Addie. I want you to look at me."

She did, her gaze held by his as he slid into her, rocking against her until she arched and cried out. Over and over, like waves crashing against the beach, her body responded.

She hadn't known pleasure like that since her first husband, and never so intense.

In that moment, she realized she'd love Russell Holt forever. And longer…

A moan escaped her, and she woke with a start, realizing she was still in the jail cell. Her heart fell at the emptiness that surrounded her. No Russ. No lovemaking, just a bare cell.

A soft snore met her ears and she sat up. There was Eef, sitting upright in a chair pulled close to the bars, head dropped onto her chest. Keeping watch. Taking care.

They had been through a lot together over the years. Addie had offered her a job as a cook after her husband had been killed, thinking she was doing the woman a favor. But instead, she'd found a friend, a true sister who could read her mind and looked after Addie and the girls as if they were her own kin.

Her heart gave a tender squeeze, and she blew a kiss at her snoozing friend before putting her head back onto the pillow.

Chapter Eight

A cold, bright moon lit the clear skies above Wylder, leaving shadows along the snow-covered ground. Russ cursed the wind as he waited outside the back entrance of the Wylder Hotel. He'd been watching for hours and a short time ago, Elliott Charles wandered outside, heading across the road with two men alongside him. They'd made their way to the Five Star Saloon.

That told him a couple of things. First, the counterparts Charles had been searching for in the train wreckage had fared well. And second...well, he was about to see what he could find out for himself.

There had to be some reason the bastard had been partnering with Clancy Willowby over the ownership of The Wylder County Social Club. What was the real interest in the club anyway? Addie made a right good living, and the place was kept up well, but it was nothing special. True, it was one of the fancier buildings in Wylder, but its location across the tracks wasn't anything special. So why the fuss? Why the challenge to Addie's ownership? The man was obviously of means with his fine clothing and fancy horse.

As best as Russ could recall, Farley Willowby wasn't any good at business or making money and neither was his brother. Coupl'a parasites as far as he was concerned. Addie had built the place up with her own hard work and efforts. So, Farley had partnered with his brother on the original purchase. Never a good thing, to borrow money, in his opinion. But why had Clancy returned after all these years? Not that the sorry bastard could answer for himself now.

He pulled the pocket watch from inside his coat. Almost nine. He pushed the small clock back into his shirt and gave a shiver. Colder than an icy dive into the river staying out this long. A click sounded at the door, and he stepped back into the shadows. The hotel kitchen help brought out the night's trash in buckets about this time and now was the chance he needed.

A young man, along with the chef both carried a bucket each to place in the alley beside the hotel. As they chatted with each other and turned the corner he trotted to the back door and eased inside. No one waited on the other side, so he made his way to the back stairs the staff used.

Given the Wylder Hotel had only one large suite for those wealthy enough to make the request, he didn't need to ask which room Charles occupied. He made it up several flight of stairs, two at a time, hoping no one stopped to question him.

As he reached the top floor, his feet sinking into the fancy carpeting, a conversation from the other end of the hall halted him. He stepped behind a planter that held a tree. Who the hell put a tree inside a place of business anyway? He touched a leaf. Damn thing was real.

The muffled female voice faded with a slam of the door and the scuffle of men's boots back down the stairs. Well, that hadn't ended well for the hopeful man, he thought with a chuckle. He eased his way to the middle door where he hoped to find the suite empty with Charles and the other men out to their drinks. He twisted the doorknob and it clicked to a stop. Locked.

He pulled the knife from his belt and dug into the edge of the wood at the catch, trying to work the connection loose.

"Sir, might I help you?"

A bell hop, of all the damn luck. And a young lad he didn't know. Russ tucked the knife behind him as he turned. He laid on a play of thick words taking a step and rocking as if he were on a drunk, he knew well. "I've the wrong…room it seems, got turned around a bit."

The lad moved closer, tipping his tiny little hat. "Let me know, sir, and I can assist you to find your way."

"No, no…" Russ gave a loud burp and slurred his words as he pulled a coin from his trouser pocket. "I'll find my way. Go on back to your duties."

The bell hop took the coin with a smile and continued on his way.

Russ waited until he was gone before pulling his knife again. The doorknob clicked on his first attempt. He slipped inside. All was quiet. A good damn thing he supposed. Time wasn't on his side, and he needed to hurry.

Lamps remained lit on tables all around the main room. He kept a firm grip on the knife, peeking in each of other two rooms that held beds. Clear. He entered the first bedroom noticing a pile of papers on a stand by the bed. He sifted through them, careful to keep them in the same order as he'd found them. Nothing of interest.

Banking papers and receipts for purchases of food.

He walked to the closet chest, rummaging through the trousers and jackets hanging there. A right good collection of fine clothing. None of the garments would have come cheap, so why would a man that wealthy give any interest to the social club?

He smoothed a hand over a smoking jacket and stopped at a filled pocket. He withdrew a derringer. The small gun was lined with crystals and gold etchings and made of a smooth black metal. Nifty if nothing else and heavy.

He studied the small weapon for a moment and lifted it to his face, inhaling near the barrel. "Huh." He muttered and sniffed again. A clean, oiled gun would smell like oil. But this one smelled like powder. Burnt powder. This gun had been fired in the past few days if he knew anything about it.

Well, from what he'd heard, Clancy had been stabbed. But a fired gun? That was interesting, now, wasn't it? Who had Charles shot with it? He took a handkerchief from his pocket, paused to trace the small, embroidered initials Addie had sewn there so long ago, and wrapped the derringer in it and tucked it into his coat pocket. The dainty cloth a reminder Addie was still in jail as he tried to figure things out.

He hurried to the next room, which held nothing but a suitcase on the bed. He flipped open the lid, finding nothing but clothing inside. Most likely, clothing that belonged to Clancy Willowby, since he was staying in the same suite. But sifting through the contents proved nothing.

He went back to the main room spying a desk across the way near the windows. He pulled open drawers, flipping through various papers. Deeds, receipts, and other papers. He thumbed through the book, the numbers in dollar funds tracked in neat penmanship but designated by various letters that didn't make words. Banking it seemed and in rather large numbers.

He pushed through another pile of papers, found a letter, then scanned it. The same letter Addie had received…explaining her to pay or hand over the social club. What the hell was that all about? Pay up or forfeit. If they wanted the club why not just take it? Why hem and haw around for a pay off? And then Addie had gone to make the pay off and Clancy had turned her down. Things weren't adding up.

He shuffled through the rest of the stack and stopped as he found a paper with ink signatures. Elliott Charles along with a Dewayne Jeffries and a Ronald Glenn. He read further. The Wylder County Social Club was listed as the place of business and shared ownership was listed with those having a signature. Now why would the ownership papers already be signed and not contain a bill of sale or include Clancy Willowby's name?

Well, that smelled of a fox in the henhouse.

He flipped through more pages but voices at the stairs stopped him. He snagged the letter and the ownership deed and shoved them into his coat. He eased the door open to the hallway and slipped from the room as Charles and his cronies reached the top of the stairs. Damn too slow. He put on his drunk act again and began weaving, singing a slurred song.

"Camp town races…sing…along…doo da." He sang at the top of his voice, smiling and tipping his hat at the men. He staggered toward them, bumping into the one who lingered behind Charles.

"Oh, sorry 'bout that, sir." He dusted the man off and kept talking. "Got myself all turned around...how d'ya get out of here?" He bobbled toward the stairs. "You gentleman have yourself a fine evening, yes sirree." He stumbled on purpose as he reached the stairs and continued singing. "Doo da...doo da."

"Drunkard." Elliott sneered.

When he reached the next level, he sped down the stairs two at a time, landing in the kitchen. The cook's shouts echoed behind him as he bolted back out into the cold, the papers and gun he'd taken weighing heavy in his coat pocket.

With any luck, the information he found would keep Addie from a noose.

Chapter Nine

The banging of the door and a rush of cold air startled Addie awake. Her body still remembered the dream she'd just had, though, and deep between her legs was the ache of unfulfilled yearning.

Damn you, Russell.

She shook the sensation off and sat up, noticing that the deputy had left at some point.

"Mornin', Adelaide," Aoife greeted, bringing with her the yeasty aroma of fresh biscuits and sausage gravy. "Sorry I'm late, Emerald is havin' an awful time with the mornin' sickness, I couldn't leave the poor thing til she perked up a bit."

Addie's stomach rumbled as the breakfast aroma wafted toward her. "She's lucky to have you. Give her my best, and tell her I'm thinking of her." She rose and headed to the bars. "You're sure a sight for sore eyes this mornin', Eef."

"Well then, your eyes are about to feel even better." As Aoife spoke the door opened again, and Pearl and Eliza came through.

Her heart lifted at the sight of them. Eliza stepped up to the bars and grabbed her hands. "Oh, Mother. This is just such an awful mess."

For the next several minutes, while Eef puttered around at the little stove in the sheriff's office warming breakfast and making tea, Pearl opened the bag she'd brought with her and began to rummage through it. She pulled out a hammer and dragged the sheriff's chair over toward the door. She stood on it, balancing as she hammered a nail into the wall and hooked a strand of pine garland over it.

Addie listened intently as Eliza filled her in on what was happening back at the social club. The blizzard still had most of the townsfolk stranded in place. Coyote was struggling to get to everyone who needed medical care and, since there was no business being done at the Club, it had been turned into a makeshift hospital and the girls were pitching in with nursing care wherever needed.

While it was comforting to know her, place was being put to good use when folks were in need, she couldn't help the nagging thought this whole situation was costing her money. Even if roads were unpassable, she knew her clientele well enough to know a few of them would have ventured to the club by now, blizzard or not.

"I've just never seen Coyote so exhausted, Mother. I worry for him." Her daughter's face brightened. "But, Mother, you must meet the nuns that are staying with us. Oh, they've been wonderful, they help with the wounded and the cooking and cleaning and the baby…"

"Baby?"

Eliza sighed. "Yes, the poor little thing. Her mother was on the train and didn't survive. Just a tiny little one. We've all taken to her, the girls take turns sitting with her and feeding and changing her. She's our own little beacon of hope in all of this. We've named her Arabella."

Addie smiled as her daughter went on about the

infant, her face alight with happiness. Eliza Jane may have come a bit late to marriage and motherhood, but it suited her like feathers suited a duck.

"The sheriff says after the town is back to normal from this storm, he will wire the railroad offices to try and find out who she was traveling with or if she has any family."

She looked up as Eef passed a cup of tea to her through the bars. "What do you think about this whole situation, Eef? Nuns and babies in the social club?"

Aoife folded her hands in front of her. "I think, Adelaide Willowby, that I am wearin' my fingers out runnin' my beads prayin' for you. Somethin' has to change. And soon."

Addie took a sip of the tea, relieved to taste honey and lemon rather than brandy, as was Eef's preference. "You know I ain't a prayin' woman, so thank you, Eef, for doin' it on my behalf."

"The nuns have been having group prayers throughout the day, Miss Addie," Pearl said from across the room. "You'd be surprised how many people are praying for you." She climbed down from the chair and dragged it over to another spot, almost in front of the door, then resumed hammering.

"I'll bet not as many as you think," Addie scoffed, taking another sip of tea. "Half of 'em are just showing up to nose around."

Eliza shook her head. "People are still snowed in. Coyote can't even get out of town to check on his patients."

Pearl was about to climb down again when the door opened, and Sheriff Wylder came through.

"What the—"

The chair wobbled, and she grabbed hold of his shoulders to steady herself.

"Well, howdy," she greeted with a wide grin before stepping down.

"What the devil are you doing?" he growled.

"Making this place a little more cheerful," Aoife spoke up. "It's downright dismal in here. Adelaide is used to noise and activity and people around—"

"It's a jail, Mrs. McCarthy. Not the social club." The sheriff removed his hat and hung his coat on a hook near the door.

Addie looked from Aoife to the new sheriff, who seemed a bit irritable this morning. "Eef, it's okay."

"Nonsense," the Irishwoman said. "A little Christmas cheer won't do the sheriff a bit of harm, either."

"Not to worry, Sheriff, you get used to it after a while," Eliza offered with her sweetest smile. "How is your wife, by the way? Please send her my best."

Branch Wylder stalked to the stove and took up the enamel coffee pot and filled his cup.

He scowled but said nothing as Pearl dragged the chair to the next spot and hammered another nail into the wall.

Aoife took the lid from the pot on the stove and stirred. "Biscuits and gravy this mornin', Sheriff?"

"I already ate." His nose twitched with interest as she continued to stir, the aroma of her delicious cooking filling the air. "Maybe a little." He leaned a hip against his desk, frowning as Pearl draped garland over another nail.

She stepped down from the chair, then turned to scrutinize her work. "See now, Sheriff? It's just a little

Christmas cheer."

He lifted the coffee cup to his lips, took a sip—and immediately spewed it out. "What the hell is in my coffee?"

"A pinch of salt and some crushed up eggshell," Aoife replied as she dished a generous helping onto a plate. "Takes away the bitter taste."

The sheriff stalked toward the door, grabbed his coat, and put his hat back on his head, muttering something about liking his coffee bitter. He yanked open the door but turned back to face them. "See this mess is cleared out first thing after Christmas."

****

Addie paced restlessly across the jail cell. Seemed all she could do these days was fret. Fret about what was happening at her business, fret about where Russ had gotten off to—and whether or not it included whiskey. And fret about the future.

What was to become of her? What if they couldn't prove her innocence? What if she wasn't innocent?

She racked her brain once more, desperate for any memory—even the slightest shadow to return.

The jail door opened, the cheery Christmas bell the gals had hung over it jingling as a gust of cold air rushed in.

Across from her, Deputy Ferguson looked up from his desk. Eliza came through the door, along with little Samuel. Behind her was Aoife, carrying an infant she assumed was little Arabella, and Opal, dragging a small fir tree. The ladies stopped inside the door to remove their cloaks and gloves.

Eliza carried Samuel over to the bars while Aoife went to the stove to warm a bottle for the baby.

"How are you, Mother?"

"I'm doin' just fine." Tears stung at the back of Addie's eyes, but she refused to give in to them. Instead, she reached through the bars to take her grandson's soft little hand. As she did so, she noticed Opal saunter over to the desk and perch a hip on the edge. "Well, hello there, Ferg."

The deputy's ears pinkened. "What you got there, Opal?"

"A Christmas tree," she said. "I knew you wouldn't mind us bringin' Miss Addie a little Christmas cheer."

"Seems to me that's all you girls have been doing." The deputy gestured toward the wall opposite him where pine boughs were adorned with bright red ribbons. "Ain't she cheered up enough yet?"

Opal gave a little squeal of laughter and reached to brush the deputy's shoulder. "Oh Fergie, you're so funny."

Eliza turned to look at them. "Deputy, do you think we might have a few minutes alone?"

The deputy frowned. "What for?"

Eliza Jane drew herself up straighter. "My milk is letting down. Surely you can understand I would like some privacy to feed my son."

Addie hid a grin at her daughter's pious tone, that girl had a reputation in town for putting folks in their place.

The young man frowned. "I don't think the sheriff would like that."

Opal changed positions to half drape herself across the desk. From the cut of her dress Addie guessed the deputy was getting an eyeful about now. "Oh, come on, Fergie. You don't want to hear our womanly chatter, do ya?"

His face flushed a rosy shade.

"You ever been with a woman, hon?" Sugar all but dripped from her voice. "Ya know, in the biblical way? You come on by some night. Bet I can keep you good and warm."

The deputy glowered but none the less rose and reached for his coat. "You ladies better not be up to something."

Opal straightened. "Well, I aim to decorate this here little tree, I don't think that's bein' up to something."

He stalked toward the door, pausing before opening it. "Fifteen minutes, you hear? Cause I'm responsible for watching Miss Addie."

Eliza nodded. "Thank you."

The door closed behind him and Opal stifled a giggle with her hand. "Fifteen minutes for that one'd be a miracle."

Once he had gone, Eliza turned to her, blue eyes misty with concern. "Mother, are you all right? Is the sheriff treating you well?"

Addie swallowed past the lump that swelled in her throat at her daughter's concern. Just a little over a year ago, she'd have never imagined such a moment for the two of them. She wrapped her hand over Eliza's on the bar. "I'm as well as can be expected. Tell me though, what's goin' on out there? Are the trains runnin' yet?" She resisted the urge to place a hand to her throat, imaging already the noose that would be there once the tracks were clear and the circuit judge made his way to town.

"No, and it will likely be several days before they

do. Do you need anything? Anything at all?"

"God rest ye merry gentleman…" Opal sang from across the room as she tied trinkets onto the small tree with dark green ribbon. Young Samuel toddled over to her, and she scooped him up, still singing.

"Well, there is somethin', in case I don't get time to tell you again."

"Ya mustn't talk that way, Adelaide," Aoife said, her tone hushed so as not to startle the drowsy baby. "I'll confess to the murder myself 'fore I'll see ya hang."

"You're a good friend, Eef, but you know I'd never allow that." Addie sniffled. "But you come on over here, I want you to hear this, too."

Aoife stepped closer, jostling the baby who teetered on the edge of sleep.

"Before anyone takes over the club—or tries to—you need to move some things." Addie glanced between the two women. "Liza Jane, there's a carpet bag way up high on a shelf in my wardrobe filled with all sorts of cash and jewelry I been collectin' over the years."

Eliza's brows rose and she leaned closer. "Mother, exactly how much are we talking about?"

Addie shrugged. "Twenty, maybe thirty thousand."

"Lord almighty, Adelaide," Aoife gasped. "How on earth—"

"You know I don't much trust banks." Addie held up a hand. "That ain't all of it. There's a loose floorboard under my desk—ya gotta slide the desk over to see it. There's a leather satchel in there with some more cash, maybe five, ten thousand. And my book."

Eliza frowned and glanced from Aoife to Addie.

"Book? Y—you mean *the* book?"

Addie nodded. Everyone suspected she had a book where she kept track of client preferences and quirks. She liked to tell folks that was all rumors, but it wasn't.

"You gals take it. Eef, you use that money to start you a new life. Find a husband to take care of." She nodded, her mind made up more and more as she talked it out. "Eliza, you put it away for your boy and the new one ya got comin'."

Aoife sniffed and wiped at one eye. "I won't tolerate such talk. You'll be home by Christmas mornin'. The nuns and I are prayin' daily."

"I appreciate that, Eef, but just in case I don't get that Christmas miracle y'all are prayin' for, you make sure that money is long gone 'fore that sneaky low-down snake of a lawyer gets his hands on my place." She paced to the other side of the small cell, wishing she could move more than a few hundred steps in any direction. "Nuns in the Club, my girls playin' nursemaid to an infant instead of workin'—the whole damn world has lost its mind on me."

The baby began to fuss, and Aoife laid her over a shoulder and began to pat her back. "I swear on my Padraig's grave, I'll take a match to every room in the place 'fore I'll let that scoundrel have it."

Addie stopped pacing and looked up at her friend. "I 'preciate that, and lock the bastard inside while you're at it." The thought gave her the first genuine smile she'd had in days. "But I got one more place where I've stashed some goods, I need to tell ya about."

Eliza's eyes, a cornflower blue like her Daddy's, widened. "More, Mother?"

"Under the side table next to my bed. Ya gotta

move it, but there's another loose board. This one has all the documents pertainin' to ever'thing I own in this world. My bible with mine and John's weddin' date and the day he passed. And your birth, 'Liza Jane. The exact number of drops to use on the men. And some more cash."

Aoife took a step backward. "Sweet Mother Mary, it's a wonder ya haven't been robbed."

"Well, that's why Russ taught me to shoot." As the words left her lips, something teased the edges of her brain. Not just the memory of Russ teaching her, or the fancy little derringer he'd bought for her. Something else. But the moment she tried to catch it, like a firefly it flitted away.

"Mother? Are you all right?"

"Did ye remember somethin'?"

Addie frowned. "No but somethin'…somethin' is tryin' to come back, I think."

The infant began to wail in earnest and Aoife stepped over to the chair near the deputy's desk and sat, rocking the baby in her arms.

"We need to get this little one home before it gets dark," Eliza said. "And the deputy's fifteen minutes are nearly up." She reached through the bars to lay a hand on Addie's arm. "Just try to relax, and maybe the memory will come. Don't force it."

Addie nodded, though she was tempted to remind her daughter that relaxing was against her better nature. Certainly not in this place.

"You gals go on." She placed her hand over Eliza Jane's and gave a squeeze.

As her daughter stepped back, Addie looked over at her longtime friend, her face aglow as she softly crooned a lullaby to the babe. A knot twisted at her heart. Aoife had devoted her entire life to caring for others, none more so than Addie herself. If she made it through this nonsense, she'd make it up to her friend. Maybe it was time she started putting others first.

Across the room, Opal fluffed the branches on the tree while keeping track of little Sam as he toddled about. "There you go, Miss Addie. You want I should put it in the cell for ya?"

"Well, it won't fit through the bars, child," Aoife scoffed. She kept her tone hushed as she rose. Eliza hurried over to place blankets over the baby and help Aoife into her cloak.

Opal giggled and dragged the tree toward the cell. She reached into her bosom and produced a key. "Quick, 'fore Ferg comes back and realizes I took it."

As the key turned in the lock, the girl looked up at her. "You could go, Miss Addie, couldn' ya. You could find Mister Russ and be free, like he said."

The temptation to do just that was overwhelming. But no, Adelaide Willowby was no coward. Russ had vowed to get her out of this, even if they had to run and start a new life. No, she wouldn't do it, not now. That wasn't the kind of freedom she wanted, running from the law the rest of her life.

The cell creaked open enough for Opal to set the tree inside. They had just latched the door again when the sound of the deputy stamping snow off his boots came outside the door.

Opal scurried over to the desk and draped herself across it, hand propping up her head, as she often did when she sat atop the piano to entertain men. "Welcome back, Ferg," she said in her best husky voice as he stepped through the door.

He stopped short, his face flushing red before he stopped to hang up his hat and coat. While his back was to her, the girl righted herself, slipped the key under some papers on his desk. When he turned back around, she stretched like a cat having a nap in the afternoon sun, thrusting her bosom forward.

Addie grinned. Her girls sure knew how to play a man. A stab of sadness panged her. She missed her girls, her place. Her freedom. What would become of them if that rich lawyer took over? She didn't want to think about that. But for now, there was a baby who needed a home, a group of lost nuns, and a man all set to take over her club the second she fell through the floor of the hangman's gallows. She swallowed hard, resisting the urge to rub at her throat as if the noose was already there.

"Well I s'pose we best shuffle off," Opal said. "Lots of work to do at the club, and Lord knows Miss Cornelia will be barkin' orders all over the place."

With a heavy heart, Addie watched as the gals trotted off, Eliza carrying young Samuel, Aoife with the infant.

Opal gave her hand a squeeze as she passed by the cell, then paused at the door to wink and blow a kiss at the deputy. "Don't forget to come see me, Fergie. "

The young man scowled and looked down at this desk.

After the door latched, Addie sat on the cot, a wave of loneliness coming over her. She tried to focus on the tree and the joy it represented, Christmas had always been her favorite time of year. She tried to imagine how it would look lit with candles and twinkling against the window of the social club. Sure, it was smaller than the tree they normally put up, but the smell put her in mind of those memories.

"Hey," the deputy's voice carried to her. "How'd that tree get in there?"

Chapter Ten

"Pull the trigger." Russ held Addie's elbow, relieved he'd gotten her away from the social club for a few hours, at least as far as she would ride on Diablo. She didn't seem to care much for horses but then she cared little for the derringer he'd purchased for her as well. But after the night she'd blown a hole in the roof of the social club trying to use a rifle, it was time she learned how to shoot.

He'd enjoyed the ride with her arms tight around his middle.

"How loud's it gonna be?" She fidgeted to free herself from his grip. "I told you I have better things to do than learn about this gun. I don't much like guns, Russ."

"Aim ahead at the post there. It's a small fire. Won't have much kick but the day comes you need it in the social club, and you'll know what to do." He gripped her elbow again. "Go on."

She gave a hummpph, closed her eyes and squeezed the first trigger. She let out a yelp and jumped as the blast came, then she fired again by accident, the double trigger throwing her.

Russ chuckled and took control of the small weapon. "You aren't supposed to close your eyes. And don't jump like that. Hold still when you fire the thing." He handed the derringer back to her.

She turned the gun toward her to look at it. "It's still smoking."

He pushed her wrist back down. "Rule number one: never point the barrel at anyone—including yourself."

"I told you I didn't want or need a gun. I ain't gonna kill anyone." She fussed, then gave a huff and pointed toward the post fifty paces away. "Ready."

He nodded and let go of her arm with a nod.

This time she fired, but the bullet strayed, digging up dirt on the far side of the post. She still jumped and blinked but that was better.

She shaded her eyes with a hand and squinted to see in the distance. "Did I hit it?"

"No." He took the gun and loaded it again and put it back into her hand. "The thing is if you barely aim, you miss by little. Focus on it."

"Well, if I ever need it, I won't be shooting so far from who I gotta hit." She winked and held steady, her breasts rising as she pulled in a deep breath.

Well, at least the view was a nice one as he taught her. Russ waited, and the shot rang out though she missed again. "It'll take some practice like now. Once more."

She shook her head but took aim and fired. Nothing. "See I think this gun is off. Maybe it can't shoot that far." She pushed the gun back toward him.

Russ took the derringer again. Typical of Addie to challenge him rather than admit defeat. "You think so, do you?"

"I took good aim. So yes, that's what I think." She folded her arms with that enticing pout. The one he loved to kiss and taste. It was almost enough to distract him from his mission of teaching her how to defend herself.

He pulled two more bullets from his breast pocket and filled the chambers of the small gun. He stepped ahead of her and took aim and fired twice in rapid succession. The post splintered both times, and he turned back to her.

Addie's mouth fell open. "How'd you do that?"

He loaded again, and she took the weapon and stood before him. "If you can do it, I can, too. Now show me."

He chuckled. Typical Addie, she didn't like to be shown up. "Take aim. Match the tip of the gun to just above the place you want to hit. Steady. Then a slight inhale and fire."

The gun sounded, and the wood on the post cracked with a hit to the side.

"I got it, did you see that. Just like you." She danced up and down swinging the gun. "Let me try again."

He grabbed her arm pointing it away from him and the horse. "First no dancing with a gun."

She studied him as he reloaded yet again. "All right, all right. Why did you want me to do this anyway?"

He kept a hand on the gun and turned her to face him. Didn't she know? He'd made love to her now and told her he loved her. Didn't she understand he'd never loved like he loved her? "Addie…'cause I care. An awful damn lot."

She put a hand on his shoulder. "Russ?"

He stared out across the prairie, all Holt-owned land ranch as far as the eye could see. "A man don't know what love is until it's lost, and I never want to lose you. You're the only one who...makes me know I'm alive and breathing sometimes."

She gave his shoulder a tender rub and he went on.

"Watching you all this time and all the talking. It's important you know...to talk and listen. Do you think all those hours I'z talking to bore you to kingdom come?"

"No. I don't think that. I wasn't bored, Russ." She let go as he pulled away.

"No, well I wasn't just talking to fill up time. Sometimes I wanted you so bad...all I could do was wallow in my own misery, but I kept talking. 'Cause talking meant we were real. We were alive and the other night...making love to you...well you were about the most beautiful thing I ever laid eyes on, save my little girl."

She followed as he stepped away.

He glanced at her and continued. "I wanted to be so far inside you we were one...the place where I could know for that brief moment you were mine. And I know you don't want my proposal now or even later...but here we are again, something as stupid as learning this gun and all I want is to be inside you, not just your body but your mind and heart and soul. God, Addie, I never loved like this before." There, he let her know why he couldn't seem to eat or sleep. Hell, he was damn near losing his mind he was so in love with her.

"Russ...our lovemaking...it's really special for me, too," she said in a whisper.

"Look, I just want you to know how to shoot. All those men coming in the social club and all." He handed her the gun again, avoiding where his emotions were taking him. "Shoot again."

"Russ, I've not spoken my heart as I should, too afraid I suppose." She shook her head. "But I do care, I do want to hear things when you talk to me. Sometimes it's lonely at the club when the girls are all busy with clients. I think about you and pine for your company but...I don't like being dependent on a man like that. It scares me."

He held her gaze. "Woman, you aren't afraid of anything."

"Maybe I am." She turned away.

Russ took hold of her shoulders to force her back around.

She took the derringer from him and took aim once more, but not before he noticed the tears shimmered in her eyes "I'm afraid to love, let go and really love...that is until you, until you...loved me for me." She took a deep breath, steadied her hand, and fired, splintering the wood once and then again.

Russ chuckled as she turned and gave him a triumphant smile "That's my girl."

****

"Lord, you might not remember me, I ain't never been much for prayin'. Not since the night you took my John, anyway. Do ya remember that? I asked in good faith and You took him anyway." Addie stared up at the ceiling, unable to sleep over the sound of Ferguson's guttural snore. *"You and I ain't had much to say to one another since then, I s'pose."* She drew in a shaky breath. *"But if you're up there and awake and listenin', I wouldn't mind some help..."*

The jail door opened. The sun had barely been up

ten minutes, so she fully expected to see Eef comin' through the door. She sat up and turned, her heart dropping.

It wasn't Aoife.

And it wasn't Russ.

Nor the help she'd been praying for.

Cornelia stopped inside the door, meeting Addie's gaze for a moment before removing her scarf and cloak. She marched up to the desk, where the deputy still snored. "Young man," she snapped. When he didn't respond, she bent and rapped her knuckles on the desk.

The deputy jerked awake.

Addie rose and walked to the bars. "Let 'im be, Corny, he had to keep watch here all night and with the sheriff off workin' on that train wreck mess, this here boy is plumb wore out."

"Hmph." Cornelia folded her arms. "Sleeping on the job, indeed. Says a lot about the state of affairs in this town, doesn't it?"

Addie sighed. Since her sister had arrived in Wylder just over a year ago all she had done was complain. Then again, that's what she did most anywhere. "All right. I know why you're here. Come to gloat, to carry on how I'm always messin' up and you're always havin' to clean up my mess. That about the size of it?"

Cornelia's dark eyes widened. "No." She stepped closer, casting an annoyed glance over her shoulder as Ferguson's snores began again. "Actually, I was coming to apologize."

Addie couldn't help the bitter laugh that burst forth. "Apologize, huh? This where you say you're sorry then launch into a lecture on how it was my fault?"

"Adelaide, I know we have not always seen eye to eye, but I am not here to take pride in what's happened. Only to say how sorry I am for any role I may have played in leading you to this."

Why was it her sister had the ability to make her mad as a wet hornet in under a minute. "Leading me? To what?"

Cornelia leaned in, keeping her voice low. "To whatever caused you to—do what you did."

Addie wrapped her hands around the bars so hard her knuckles turned white. "You think I killed a man?"

Ferg gave a snort and shifted position.

"Well given the people you surround yourself with—"

Addie wrapped her hands around the bars, wishing for a second it was Cornelia's damn neck. "You talkin' about my girls?"

"Among others, yes. But that drunkard you keep company with isn't much of an improvement over Farley. It's good you came to your senses, it's just a shame it was too late."

Addie ground her teeth. "Cornelia, if I could reach through these bars—"

Her sister sank into the chair in front of the cell. "And that's precisely what I mean. You've always had a temper, Adelaide. Even when you were small."

"And you've always been holier than thou—even when *you* were small." She folded her arms and moved away from the bars, as far from her sister as she could get.

"I didn't come to argue. I just…" Cornelia's voice broke, and Addie turned to look over her shoulder.

"I wanted to see if there was something I could do." She pulled a handkerchief from her sleeve and dabbed it to her nose. "I just feel so helpless."

The anger that had been simmering at the surface left in a rush. "Aww, Corny. This ain't yours to fix."

She clenched the handkerchief in her fist, casting a sour glance when the deputy's snoring grew louder. "I just keep thinking if you weren't involved with that awful man, this never would have happened."

"Russ?" The anger started to simmer again. "I need to warn you, even if I did kick that man out of my club and my life, I love him and I won't tolerate anyone talkin' bad about him."

"No," Another sniffle. "Not him. The other one. That no good Farley. I disliked him from the moment I set eyes on him."

Addie let out a yelp of laughter. "That makes two of us."

Cornelia gave her a watery smile. "I just thought any man who wanted you to leave your child behind was up to no good."

"I know." She sighed. "You were right all those years ago, you warned me. But I was too stubborn to listen." She sank onto the hard, cold floor and looked up at her sister. "I wanted a new life, away from all the memories of John, and I thought it would be easier on Eliza Jane if she didn't have to get hauled around until we were settled and had our business runnin'."

Cornelia nodded. "I know."

"S'pose you knew even then it would be longer than a year, though." Addie studied her older sister. She looked older, somehow, smaller than she had just the other day. The stress of her being in here was wearing on everyone, it seemed.

She twisted the hanky between her fingers. "I hoped I was wrong, you know that."

"You were wrong about John, at least," Addie pointed out. "You told me not to marry him, but he was a good man. Would'a made a wonderful father."

Pulled from her reminiscing, Addie glanced up at her sister's face.

"I did warn you about marrying John, didn't I." Her voice was solemn. "But I didn't mean it. I…" her voice hitched again. "I was jealous, Adelaide. I'd loved John from afar for years and then he turned his attention on you. You were such a fickle little thing, I thought sure you'd throw him over and move on to someone else. But you didn't."

Her heart constricted at the memory of her late first husband. But remembering him wasn't as sad now as it once had been, the feeling was more bittersweet. "I'm sorry about John. I never knew you had feelings for him. But I loved him with all my heart." Shook off a sudden sentimental feeling.

"There's more," Cornelia said, her voice catching. "When caring for Eliza Jane proved to be more than any of my potential suitors cared to take on and my prospects dried up, I resented you. I'm sorry, Adelaide. I didn't mean to. But now I'm alone and you've taken up with that no account cowboy, and—"

Addie reached through the bars to put a hand on her sister's knee. "Russ is a good man, Corny. Give him a chance."

Cornelia raised her nose a bit. "He's a drunk and he upsets you."

She shook her head. "He upsets me because I love

him and don't want to see him drink his' self to death. He's good to me, Corny. He loves me, genuinely loves me. He aint' like Farley." She gave a small bark of laughter. "Believe me, I ain't that girl no more, naïve and hopeful. Nobody gets the wool over my eyes these days."

"Oh, Addie, what are we going to do?" Cornelia wailed. "You're the only family I have left in this world, if we don't get you out of this…" She put the handkerchief to her mouth and stifled a sob.

"We're gonna trust Russ. He said he'd get me outta this, and one way or another, he will."

****

Cold wind swirled dry snow across a midnight Wylder as Russ left the Five Star Saloon. Funny he hadn't taken even a sip of the fine purchase of bourbon he'd made. Instead, he had stared at the liquor for several hours, alone at the table in the corner.

The time spent studying the small cup of relief was needed. And now he understood a bit about what Dalton Payne had tried to tell him about always having a small flask in his vest pocket as a reminder. Maybe a man had to look at it to find himself a way free of it. He wasn't too sure that would work for him, but he hadn't touched what he'd purchased.

Ah well, he needed no more convincing not to drink that little glass. At least for now and where it came to Addie, he had to set the drink aside and not let it drown out the voices in his head. Her predicament gave him a few things to keep his mind occupied from memories that might otherwise bring him to his knees wanting that precious liquid.

He ducked his head, holding onto his hat in the

frigid gusts, glad he'd left Diablo at the livery earlier. He glanced at the jail where a bit of a dim light glowed. He needed to talk to Addie whether she liked it or not.

Branch had headed home earlier which meant Ferguson was on duty and, while the young man tried hard, he wasn't the brightest apple on the tree. So, with any luck he would find the deputy snoring as usual and wake Addie to chat if she were sleeping. He needed answers, and he had some news to share. Things were adding up where he was beginning to put a few things together.

He stepped to the door of the jail office, eased his hand to the doorknob, and turned. The click of the latch sounded. He gave a nod to himself and stepped inside, careful not to make noise with his heavy boots. He took another step and closed the door behind him with precise ease, letting the click sound.

As expected, Ferg was leaned back in the sheriff's chair, snoring loud and clear, his hat tilted across his face. He'd seen this a time or two since the new deputy had been sent from Cheyenne to work with Branch. Almost as if the sheriff of Cheyenne was pawning off the young lawman to get rid of him.

Across the room in the darkened cell, Addie rose from the cot. Her gaze met his though she didn't speak—or smile. He crept closer and urged her to follow to the far side of the cell in the shadows. She stopped before him. The bars between them might as well have held them at opposite ends of the earth.

He motioned for her to keep her voice down but then she would know that. "You stayin' warm? Seems a mite cold." It was small talk at best. How he wanted to touch her, lie with his head in her lap, and chat all night long.

"I'm plenty warm." She folded her arms, pouting. Had she not been on the other side of the bars, she might have gotten all riled up at him as usual.

"Got a lot of Christmas going on in here." He glanced at the small tree and the garland and ribbons the girls had used to decorate around the jail.

"Eef and all the girls," she whispered. Damn, he'd kill that bastard for the sadness in her sweet blue eyes.

He nodded though the weariness or fear in her eyes showed. "Got some news. I been sniffing around finding out what I can on this top hat, Charles. But Addie, you gotta tell me what you know. Anything you might add. Anything at all you can remember."

Her pout was visible even with a bit of a shadow playing across her face. "A fine time, the snow melts and I'm done for. Where've you been?"

He shook his head, looking behind him as Ferg snorted and adjusted his position. He held a hand up to stop their exchange and waited until the deputy's snoring became even again. "Got a better idea." He pointed to the floor on the side of the cell. He fell to his knees and offered his hand thru the bars.

Addie pursed her lips tight and sat on the floor beside him. He tilted his position to lean against the bars but didn't let go of her hand. She was still angry at him, he supposed.

"Don't worry, he hardly wakes for a thing. No wonder Branch doesn't leave him to do much around here." She used her other hand to straighten her skirt, always a lady.

"He won't see us as easy if we're down here." He whispered, wanting to say a lot more, but now wasn't the time.

She took in a deep breath, let it out, and glanced at their joined hands.

"What do you know about Clancy?" he asked.

She released a heavy sigh. "A foolish man with his money. I never could trust him or Farley to do the right thing."

"What about the amount of the pay off?" He held her gaze, the single lamp at the desk now let the shadows play over her skin, enticing the touch he so wanted.

"He wanted forty thousand." She shook her head. "Farley never once told me he borrowed that money. As much a no count as his brother it seems."

That was the amount listed on one of the papers he'd lifted from Charles' room. He glanced at the deputy, who hadn't moved further. "What about this Elliott Charles? When did he come into the picture?"

She pulled her hand free of his to brush her hair back. "I got the letter Eef burned and then he showed up with Clancy to town a few days before…before he was killed."

"He has two men with him now. Came in on the derailed train. The fancy car and two others at the end of the tracks didn't derail from what I can figure. Seen them with him in the saloon a couple of times now, scratched up some, but not hurt." He explained still keeping his voice soft.

She wrung her hands together. "Well now, who are they?"

He eased in a deep breath and let out a huff of air. "Near as I can figure from New York City, smelling of money. Not sure what their part in this is except…" He reached into his shirt and tugged free the papers he'd found at the hotel. Careful to open both he handed the one with Charles' and the other two men's signatures on it to her.

She read the details, then looked at him. "It's an agreement for the Social Club."

He nodded. "That doesn't include Willowby, though."

She studied the back of the paper and then the front of it again. "Wait a minute. Where'd you get this?"

"Did some shopping at the hotel and found this, too." He yielded the derringer from his coat pocket, unwrapped it, and held it out to her.

Addie drew a sharp breath. She touched the metal barrel. "Russ...I've seen that gun somewhere before. Where did you get it?"

He studied her as she touched the small gun, wide eyed. Her breathing increased and her voice wavered. "Clancy. I went to...see him—by his self, not with Charles. I figured I could pay him off and leave the other fella out of it. But that gun. Why do I remember it?"

Russ narrowed a gaze on her. "Keep thinking."

"Shhh." She waved a hand at him. I told Clancy I wanted a paper drawn up and signed for me to pay so he couldn't come back, ever. And then that lawyer fella showed up and he changed his mind. Like havin' the other feller there made Clancy bolder. That lawyer said my terms were not acceptable and he'd be taking ownership of the social club."

She continued to stare down at the derringer. "Then Clancy insisted on following me out of the hotel as if he were a gentleman. But I felt dizzy or somethin' and...I remember thinkin' I wished I'd brung Abraham, cause my knees felt all wobbly and out of sorts. Then I stumbled and my purse spilled."

"Go on."

She frowned. "I remember looking' at it all layin' there in the snow, it felt like the world was movin' so slow, but the snow was just comin' down fast and it was freezing. I bent to pick my things up—I must've fallen cause I remember goin' down on my hands and knees and thinkin' how cold that snow was. When I looked back up—Elliott Charles had that gun. It was pointed right at me, but something was wrong. My mind wasn't right, like I couldn't gather my thoughts to think clear. I don't know what happened next but at some point, the gun went off."

"So, Clancy accompanied you outside and Charles had the gun on you but shot him instead? That sums it up well enough." Russ cast another glance at the sleeping Ferg. "This gun has been shot recently, at least the first chamber. What else, Addie?"

"I don't think so. I...the gun was in my face, and I just knew he was gonna kill me, but then...Clancy fell across me. I tried to scream but no sound come out, or if it did, I didn't hear it. I don't remember anything else until Eef was slappin' my cheeks, making me walk to the carriage and Amethyst and Ruby helped me in and then...I just remember them helpin' me undress...and cleaning Clancy's blood off'a me." She clenched her fist and looked up at him with some of the Addie fire he hadn't seen in far too long. "That rat's ass bastard, thinking he'd kill me and take my club."

He grinned, happy to see the fire in her eyes again.

She looked off in the distance, as if the memories

were playing out in front of her eyes. "Then Branch come and said my letter opener was found beside Clancy at the alley behind the hotel and he arrested me. It had to be Elliott Charles killed him instead of me or leastwise he missed. My purse...the letter opener was in my purse. That's it. But I was so mixed up. I couldn't have used a gun. Frankly, I thought I was going to be sick, but Clancy fell on me and knocked me senseless, I was just so ill..."

Well, that explained plenty. Russ nodded. "Sounds like it won't take much to figure this one then. Did you drink anything at the hotel when you were talking to Clancy?"

She shrugged. "Yes, he offered me a scotch but..."

He had an idea or two about this. "Did it feel like you were walking in slow motion...a bit dizzy..."

Her eyes turned wide and unassuming. "Why yes..."

"I believe, madam, you've been given a taste of your own medicine." He chuckled keeping it to a whisper. "You said Clancy was at the social club prior to when he was killed?"

"Yes and Cornelia ran him off. But..." she stopped her mouth dropping open. "That rotten bastard. He took a cup at the social club and used it on me." She trembled, her voice growing louder. She rose to her feet as if a sudden burst of energy made it impossible to keep still.

He cranked himself up beside her reminding her to be quiet with a finger to his lips as Ferg snorted and grumbled.

"That rotten scoundrel...they planned it all. Gave me the drink so Clancy thought he could shoot me but then Elliott Charles got him out of the way so he could get my club all to himself. That's the reason for him and his men being the only ones on this deed." She scowled and handed the paper back through the bars. "I've been shafted. And not in a good way a'tall."

The deputy woke and jumped to attention. "Hey, you aren't supposed to be in here talking to the prisoner." He scrambled to get out of the chair and right his hat.

"It's all right. I'm leaving." Russ glanced back at Addie who cursed a streak under her breath.

"Wait!" she called as he turned to wave. "You gotta let me out of here. Ferg, I'm not guilty, you have to let me out so I can prove it."

Russ reached inside the bars, took her hand, and brought it up to kiss it. "I'll be back. You stay here."

"No. I don't wanna stay here another damn second." She wouldn't let go of his hand, tugging as he tried to pull free. "Russell Holt, you get me out of here."

He turned again, staring at her meaningfully. "Addie, stay put. If you're here Charles' men can't get to you, and neither can he."

She grabbed the bars, yanking. "Well, that's a fine how do ya do. I don't care if I'm safer in here."

Ferg cleared his throat. "You gotta go, Mr. Holt."

Russ gave a nod to Addie, though her expression made it clear she wasn't having it. "Russ, don't you leave me in here."

He turned to the deputy. "Listen, son. We just figured out what happened to Miss Addie. I can free her of the charges, and I'll prove it to Branch. But your job's gonna be most important. You gotta guard her with your life."

"Well yes, sir." Ferg seemed to stand a little taller as he glanced from him to Addie and back. "But the sheriff..."

"Ferg. This could be the highlight of the year for a deputy like yourself. The one who kept an eye on the Madam that's gonna be set free of the crime. Your name will be in all the papers, and people will want to know what's happened and how you helped." Russ turned and winked at Addie. Lord, she was gonna kill him dead once and for all.

"Really?" the young man beamed a grin. "You really think so?"

"Sure. You kept her safe from the one who did the crime. I can see it on the front of the papers now." Russ didn't share the names. He didn't need any bit of this information in the wrong hands.

Ferg leaned closer. "But who is that? The real one?"

"Can't say yet." Russ stepped toward the door.

Addie yanked on the bars. "Russ, you cannot leave me in here another day. So help me I will..." Her voice echoed behind him as he slipped out the door. He almost felt sorry for Ferg, knowing he'd take the brunt of Addie's tantrum...though he'd have his own hell to pay about this later, but if his suspicions were right, it might just be worth it.

Chapter Eleven

Addie shivered and pulled her cloak tighter.

Heading out in this blinding snow at this hour of night was not a good idea. But after the hell of a day she'd been through, it was the least of her worries.

Tossing Russ out hadn't been easy, but his alcohol consumption had taken a toll on both of them. It was time to let him go. Though breaking her own heart hadn't been part of the plan.

Then Abraham had asked to marry Emerald. Oh, she hadn't been surprised about that a bit, but it would change things for her and the girls at the club. And what if he left for a more respectable job, one that wouldn't keep him from home at night? It wasn't as if she could keep some of those big cowboys from causing trouble all on her own. And now without Russ…she sighed.

"Well, if I don't get this sorted out then I won't have a social club to worry about." She trudged ahead, leaning into the wind, protecting her eyes with a single hand over her face. Her fingers were near frozen in the short walk to the Wylder Hotel where, in spite of her misgivings, she intended to talk to Clancy Willowby.

She'd offer him a sum all his own—apart from his slimy partners—to go away and let this be the end of it. The letter had said she could pay or forfeit the club to his ownership. Well, over her dead body would she ever let him have the business she'd built.

She grabbed onto the railing at the steps of the Wylder Hotel and made her way up to the port. As she pushed through the main doors, the wind sucked the large door to a slam behind her, a shower of flurries following her inside. She dusted her coat and shuffled her boots across the welcome rug.

"Miss Addie, what on earth are you doing out in the cold?" The hotel clerk whispered. Addie took in a warm breath and removed her head scarf before facing the young man. "Yes, well, I should say I've had better days for such a visit, but I've need to speak with Mr. Clancy Willowby, I believe he is staying here."

He nodded toward the stairs. "Yes, ma'am, he's on the top floor suite. Room one, on the third floor."

Addie gave him a smile and headed toward the stairs. She removed her gloves and unbuttoned her cloak with still frozen fingers as she began the haul to the third floor. She'd been in the hotel numbers of times, most often to negotiate or collect funds upfront from high paying clients that preferred one of the girls to visit them inside the hotel. Such a way of conducting business wasn't her preference, but it paid well.

The thick carpet made for a luxurious walk to the top of the stairs on the third floor. She took a deep breath and glanced, straightened her cloak, hoping the matter didn't take long. Clancy Willowby, had always been a weasel. But paying him off might prove to run him and that businessman right out of Wylder.

She was certain they had no idea that she had the money. None around her, including Eef, were aware how much she'd stashed away over the years. She only kept a small percentage in the bank, not all of it. Though she hadn't brought the cash with her tonight, she had come to strike a deal instead. It was a given neither Clancy nor his counterpart could be trusted and if they agreed, she'd have the bank deliver the draft when they drew up the paperwork for her to sign.

She stopped before the door and took a deep breath. She still had no idea what Farley might have promised or signed away to his younger brother. Neither of them had a mind for anything but trouble. If she hadn't been so grief stricken over losing John, she never would have married Farley. Oh, he'd had his good points, but they had been few and far between. But he'd done her a favor the night he'd risen from a game of cards in the saloon, clutched his chest, and keeled over dead.

She reached the door, hesitated a moment to gather her nerve, and knocked.

The door swung open and before her stood Clancy's partner, Elliott Charles. Anger skittered down her spine at the sight of him. He lifted his brows. "Mrs. Willowby, what a pleasant surprise."

"A word with Clancy, please." She had no time for the man's smooth attempts at formalities.

As she stepped inside, he backed up. "By all means." Bowing elegantly, he allowed her to pass.

Clancy rose from the small desk on the opposite side of the room and faced her. "Adelaide?"

Well, she supposed there was no need to beat around the bush. She glanced at Charles, who moved in beside her. "I've just ordered and received a fresh pot of tea, would you care for a cup? It's a blustery night out there, surely you could do with warming yourself by the fire."

"Yes, Addie, come closer to the fire, what on earth,

out in this?" Clancy, who hadn't a decent bone in his body didn't fool her by feigning his concern. All he'd ever cared about was himself.

But the heat beckoned to her, and she moved closer to the small fireplace, taking the cup of tea Mr. Charles handed over. She sipped and then held his gaze. "I would like a moment to speak to Clancy alone."

The man's dark eyes flickered with anger, though he quickly covered it with a curt smile that reeked of insincerity. "Certainly, madam."

Addie waited as he took his coat from a stand near the door and left the room. She turned her sights on Clancy. Lord, he was as short and stout as she remembered. "This won't take long." She began as he motioned her to sit and take a place on the settee. She took another sip of tea, frowning at the faintly bitter taste, and set it aside. "I will get right to the point."

Clancy folded his arms. "You've come about the letter."

The jackass shouldn't play dumb now. "I am ready to put an end to this, Clancy. But on my terms."

He shook his head. "Addie…"

"I will pay you and only you to go away and never bother me again over the social club which you know good and damn well is mine. Mine!" She shouted at the same time her thoughts seemed to fray and her head spun with a slight dizziness. She grabbed the nearby table to steady herself. "I want it drawn up legal, from the local law office."

Clancy stepped forward, rubbing his balding head. "Addie, we've, uh, we've had a change in plans, as Elliott and I prefer to keep the club as opposed to taking my fair half of the payment for it."

Addie's pulse raced. What was he saying? "Clancy, I've the money in full to pay you in cash, but you have to leave here and take that Charles with you."

He chuckled then as if any of this was funny. "You don't understand, we no longer want any money. Come first of the year, we'll be taking over the social club in full."

Addie gritted her teeth. "You only have the rights to the half of what belonged to you."

"No, I'm afraid…" He turned back to the desk and picked up a piece of paper flailing it in front of her. "We've spoke to our lawyers in New York and received this deed of which shows my full ownership beginning January first. It's legal, sweet Addie, and there's not a thing in the world you can do to stop us."

"That is my place." She gestured to her chest. "I built it with my hard work while Farley played games and gambled money away. If part of the club was yours, where the hell were you all this time?"

A smug grin crossed his features, then blurred.

She blinked, her thoughts swirling in circles, and it felt like an effort just to speak. "Over my dead body. I was willing to pay you enough to haul your sorry hind end out of Wyoming and crawl back under whatever rock you slithered out from. But now." She put a hand to her head as the room began to spin.

He laughed, the sound echoing around her. Her legs and arms began to feel heavy. Something wasn't right. She needed to get out of here—quick. "I will see you in hell, Clancy Willowby."

She took up her cloak and scarf and strode toward the door, pulling it open so hard it banged against the wall and stepped into the hallway. A flash of heat flushed through her. She hadn't been this angry in a long time. She adjusted her cloak over her arm and decided not to bother wearing it, at least not just yet.

As she made it to the stairs, she grabbed hold of the railing as her knees began to wobble together. Clancy followed behind her, catching up to her just as she reached the front door. "Addie, wait, let me walk you back you shouldn't be out in this weather." He half ran to catch up to her, slipping and sliding in the rapidly falling snow.

She turned and shouted against the weather "I don't need help from the likes of you," she called over her shoulder. "I can find my own way home."

He stayed close to her as they crossed the street. Addie's mind blurred and she stumbled, spilling the contents of her bag to the snow-covered ground. She stopped, the numbing cold and blowing snow confusing her further. She couldn't make one clear thought. As she bent to pick up her purse Elliott Charles appeared before them.

"What's going on?" he snapped, dark gaze darting from her to Clancy.

"She wants to pay me off, but I told her, no...wait, what..." Clancy tugged at her arm. She resisted, though it seemed to take a lot of effort just to pull away.

The taller man laughed, and she glanced up to find that her former brother-in-law had a derringer pointed at her. She opened her mouth to scream, but the hiss of the wind rushed in her ears. Clancy had hold of her arm. She slipped, nearly dragging him down with her.

The other man stepped closer, his dark shoes a stark contrast to the snow.

Clancy looked over his shoulder. "Elliot," his voice

sounded panicked. "Wait, what're you—"

A blast echoed into the night, Clancy fell, landing atop her, flattening her into the cold snow. Her face stung from the cold, and her lungs struggled to take in enough air with his weight on her. She wanted to scream but couldn't draw enough breath.

And then blackness swallowed her whole.

Chapter Twelve

The air hung stale and cold as Russ made his way to the Social Club. The midnight chat with Addie had proven enough for him to take a look in her office and bedroom. But even with her memory of the events beginning to surface, he wasn't sure what he was looking for.

Addie was safer in jail whether she like the idea or not. She could fuss at him later but in case Elliott Charles had a mind to take out Addie next, he had Ferg keeping a better eye on her. Well, at least now the young deputy had a purpose for the gun he wore strapped to his hips and thigh.

Russ suspected Clancy had been going to kill Addie all along, which was his reason for escorting her outside the hotel. He was no gentleman. He had either been planning to kill her or his counterpart Charles had been going to do it.

But now he had to figure out how Clancy was shot. Did Charles point the gun at Addie and then turn it on Clancy? Or had he missed hitting Addie in the confusion?

And he hadn't a doubt she had been given some of her own recipe from the Social Club. The question became how did Clancy Willowby or Elliott Charles get the concoction, but how did either man know of the secret kept inside the social club?

He crossed the tracks on foot and eyed the social club from a distance. Somehow the large three-story oversized home now seemed lost without its Madam. He chuckled. And she would be lost without it.

Ice crunched under his boots as he made the stairs two at a time. He pushed open the front door and stepped inside. A lamp was on each table and the room held its after-hours glow, though Christmas décor was all over, and people were scattered about the floor on makeshift bedding.

Others lay in beds that had been lined together, those recovering from the train derailment. He'd expected to be met by Abraham but the oversize freeman, if not watching the door was one place. With Emerald. He chuckled, though he did a quick scan for Coyote, since the injured were housing here in the club, though it did seem things were quiet considering.

Whispers and giggles echoed from the floors above as he stepped down the small hallway to Addie's office. In the darkness he bumped a small tree and bells jingled making him curse under his breath.

Shit. He held the branches still as not to turn the bastard over. It was almost Christmas so he should have expected the decor change, though it had shocked him the jail held just as much by the way of a tree and ribbons and garland. The girls always did the place up nice. He peeked into the second room, the one where multiple settees hosted men waiting their turn. Nuns lined the wall on one large palate across the far wall. He shook his head. Addie wouldn't much be fond of that.

He stepped into Addie's office and fumbled to find a match to light the small lamp on her desk. He fanned the match out and let his eyes adjust to the glow.

Nothing was out of place. Neat and in order. Stacked items on her desk. He picked up a pile of papers on the edge of the desk and sifted through. Bills from Lowery's Dress Shoppe and some from one of the local bakeries. A carriage repair bill from the livery and a list of things to do. He set the stack back down and opened the side drawers to the desk.

At the creak of a floorboard, he stilled, his hand going to his revolver.

Cornelia stood in the doorway holding a small candle on a plate. "I thought I smelled a mouse in the cupboard."

Russ stifled a curse.

"Russel Holt, you've no business here especially with the absence of Adelaide, though if she were here I'd tell you both the same."

He let out a breath. Of all the luck he might have expected. "Cornelia, you should know not to startle a man wearing a gun." Of course, the likes of Addie's older sister might scare a corpse from its grave if it came down to it. He forced a smile. "Do you know where she keeps the powders or a list of visitors to the club?"

She set the candle aside and placed her hands on her hips. "No, and if I did, I wouldn't be sharing it with the likes of you."

He paid her no mind and opened another drawer pulling out a ledger. He thumbed through it. Names of businesses in town but nothing more than dates and figures in Addie's penmanship.

"I'll have Abraham toss you out on your ear," she threatened. "It's not enough I had to be rid of that Clancy Willowby and his counterpart, but I also had to

119

run that Cade Anson right off...him bringing flowers for Aoife as though a woman her age has any interest in courting him."

The woman rambled on as she adjusted her night robe up to her neckline. Hell, he hadn't ever had a thought of that...he gave a shiver.

Aoife stepped into the room a blush across her cheeks. "Cornelia, please."

Russ caught the reason for Eef's rose colored cheeks. It was no secret Cade had been interested in Eef for some time now, she was a fine-looking woman. But she was too devoted to Addie to even consider his attentions.

"I caught Mr. Holt breaking and entering as we speak." Cornelia spoke in a whispered huff.

"Wait." Russ stopped both ladies by holding up a hand. "When was Clancy here?"

Eef stepped closer as Cornelia answered. "Well, the night of his murder."

"No. What did he do when he was here?" Russ waved a hand again. "Wait, did you say Elliott Charles was here with him?"

"Yes." Eef nodded and gave Cornelia a scalding glare.

He figured Cornelia not to be of much help, but Eef would know his only interest was saving Addie. He raised his brows, waiting.

"He must've been watching for Abraham to be sent out for errands aye, and he and Mr. Charles came inside and would take no for an answer as they made their way into this office," Eef explained, and she pulled her night robe tighter.

Cornelia folded her arms and pressed her lips tight.

Well, she was often scandalized by his presence. So be it.

Russ stepped closer to Eef. "Where was Addie at the time?"

"Well, she was with Abraham. A short visit to pick up a few things from the mercantile what with that being the night the storm was blowing in on us."

Russ shut the drawer. "Where does Addie keep the powders for the men's drinks?"

"Men's drinks?" Cornelia tsked him. "I should say to a man like you there is no alcohol allowed at the Social Club."

Upstairs the baby began to cry.

Aoife placed a hand to Cornelia's shoulder. "The baby's due her nightly feeding. Could you see to it?"

The woman wasn't easily persuaded. "Aoife, we can hardly share information with Mr. Holt... given...well given Addie is jailed."

Eef lifted her brows. "Cornelia, like it or not Russ is our only hope. Now please see to the wee one."

With a last huff of exasperation Cornelia headed for the door. "I'd sooner kiss a sow on the street than assist that man at anything."

Russ couldn't help a grin. "I can arrange that sow any time you're ready, Corny." He used Addie's pet name for her intentionally to rile her even further. Her indignant shriek as she walked away was all the reward he needed.

"Russ." Eef shook her head. It wasn't the first time he and Cornelia had disagreed and it likely wouldn't be the last.

"That woman..." He bit his tongue.

Eef placed a finger to her lips and walked to the

corner of the room. He got up to follow her to a bookshelf built into the walls. She pulled free one of the larger books and laid it on the shelf, opening it.

Russ leaned closer. The thick book had been hollowed out. Inside were tiny pouches with vials of liquid. He lifted one. He'd seen the bottles before but never where they'd been kept.

"Addie keeps the supply here. None of the girls know where the main supply is, myself included. But enough is kept here for a few days." Eef pointed to another of the books. "Addie moves things from time to time. She gets the drops from the apothecary, I suspect."

Russ dropped the pouch back inside and Eef replaced the book. "She'll find out I told ya and move them again. She's a woman of purpose and means."

"That she is." Russ turned. "When Clancy and Charles were here, did they discover this?"

"I can't prove it, but I suspect so. They shoved us all out and bolted the door for a time." Eef shook her head. "Course I had a key and Cornelia and I ran them off. But the books were out of order so I'm afraid it's quite possible."

"Thanks, Eef." He adjusted his hat. "Sorry to disturb things, wake you all and the little one."

She tsked. "If you're looking to save Addie, Russ Holt, then I'm abiding to you. And the little one upstairs is warm and dry and fed thanks to you, though I do wish we knew who the poor soul belonged to. We've named her Arabella."

He stopped at the door and gave her a smile and stepped into the hallway but then turned back to her. "If you don't mind my saying, Eef. Cade's a damn good man. No drinkin' or a cussin'…reads that bible of his quite regular."

A blush filled her cheeks so fast they resembled plump apples. "Go on along, Russell Holt. I've no need for another man since my Paddy."

Russ found his way outside the social club with proof now that Clancy had known about the drops. It was odd that he would have known about them, so someone must have had leaked that to him.

But it was of little importance now, all that mattered was getting Addie the hell out of jail.

****

The late spring sun hung bold in the morning sky, searing Wylder with the first hints of a long hot summer. Russ picked up his hat to drag an arm across his sweaty brow and placed the hat back on his head. He turned to his horse about the time he saw her.

She flitted along, crossing the street in a flurry of skirts. Pale blonde hair arranged beneath a fancy hat that lent height to her petite frame, a tiny waist and the kind of curvaceous hips that made a man forget himself. The madam of The Wylder County Social Club was in a hurry, as she always was the few times he'd seen her when he was in town.

Unaware or uncaring of his ogling, she disappeared inside Lowery's Dress Shop. She returned a short time later with ladies' clothing draped over her arm. He removed his gloves one at a time and watched her as she began the walk back across the tracks.

She nodded to patrons and greeted the other women with a pleased "good morning" as she passed them, but few snuffed her a response. He supposed she was used to that, but she kept her head high and went on about her business as if unbothered by their reactions. Such was the life of a Madam, not real popular among the ordinary women in town. But she was no whore, not Addie, though she ran a tight ship for the girls that did the whorin'. Men up to no good didn't last long either, she kicked them out on their hind ends.

Addie carried herself like she was the shiniest penny on any street she should walk, in spite of what others thought. Graceful and sure of herself. That's what he'd first noticed about her.

He put his latest purchase of skinny cigars in a small tin right next to the glass bottle of bourbon inside his saddle bags. He lifted the bottle and turning away from the street sucked down a small hit of the alcohol. Just enough to steady his hands. Enough to keep him calm and focused.

He turned once more to glance down the road, but Miss Addie—as most referred to her—had disappeared from view. Ah, it was just as well, but he'd decided in that moment to make her his wife one of these days. Though it was something he'd yet to tell her and something he'd have to mind his fences about.

But what few saw was that she ran a business just like any other merchant in the small town of Wylder. The brothel stayed rather busy from his viewpoint, and he had an idea or two about that as well. He sucked in a deep breath, closed his saddle bag, and mounted up on the gelding he'd just purchased.

The weekend was coming. Saturday night he was going to head to the social club and see just how things might transpire. He had no interest in the whores if the truth were to be told, but he'd come to a long-time conclusion that conversation with a woman was sometimes of more pleasure than what most men went to the club for.

He chuckled. And he might have to talk a mile or more to make his way to the Madam. But the way it seemed his life was going, he had plenty of time to be patient about it.

He clicked his tongue and urged the horse outside of town where the work waited. Assuming his role back on the ranch he'd shared with his brother hadn't come easy, and the ghosts that haunted his past were better off put to rest with the drink on most Saturday nights.

He turned the horse back and headed toward the tracks. It was early morning. Most men visited the club in the late evenings. He let the horse amble along until the rail was behind them and the social club came into view, wanting one more glance of her.

The white clapboard, three story structure sat outside the main town as if an eye sore to the citizens, though it was anything but that. Whomever had built the place hadn't spared a penny on its appearance. Splashed a white paint with red shutters and a tin roof, there were even flowers in the planters and rockers on the porch.

As he rounded closer, Miss Addie was on the porch having words with one of the ladies who worked inside with the cooking and cleaning. Both glanced up at him and he tipped his hat and rode on by…for now.

He'd return Saturday and visit the social club. Any woman would do for starters as he was planning to talk…just talk. Paying for a woman's conversation would earn him a place inside the club to see how best to work his way to the Madam.

Yep, that's just what he'd plan to do. Talk his way to Miss Addie. Then one day when they were accustomed to each other and he discovered what she held inside that mind of hers...well, then he might enjoy finding himself deep inside her with her legs wrapped tight around him as they both found their bliss. But for the time being...he'd talk and learn all he could about her.

He chuckled and circled the horse back outside of town to head to the ranch, a vision of the Madam naked beneath him a bit too much. He urged the horse to a hard gallop to toss his mind away from his thoughts for the time being. But come Saturday...yeah, come Saturday.

Chapter Thirteen

Russ opened one eye and blinked. A deep brown eyeball stared back at him. A loud giggle came before it ducked away and returned again. Had his head not pounded like a black powder explosion he might have chuckled. He closed his eyes again not ready to face the morning, at least not until he had a cup of coffee or another hard swallow of rot gut. He growled.

"It's morning, Grandpa. You gettin' up?" Jesse, his five-year-old grandson popped up by his bed, his words holding a hint of his mother's British accent. "But now the train rode off the tracks. Pa says town's one big mess in the snow. You ever seen a train off the tracks, Grandpa?"

Russ rolled from his belly to his back and closed his eyes with a hard grumble.

Well, that wasn't all that was a total mess.

After he'd ransacked Elliott Charles' room the night before, he'd hung in the saloon for a few hours sucking down enough bourbon to steady his hands. He'd told himself it was to take the edge off but given the headache he had this morning, he'd gone a little further than that.

There were times it just wasn't easy to think about giving up the only thing that helped.

"Not but the once. And I'm getting up here in a minute." He answered not wishing to explain his knowledge of the train's derailment and thinking an instant death might be easier for himself.

He'd spent time talking to Coyote last night, who scolded his having a drink even if it was to calm his shaking hands and keep his nerves steady while he worked to find a way to set Addie free. But the Doc and Eliza had been up to their own digging. They had telegrammed some contacts in New York, and it seemed Jeffries and Glenn were known smugglers who had a number of counts riding against them.

Russ had filled Sullivan in on what he knew about the whole situation and had the physician on board to help with what he had to do next.

"It's almost Christmas, Grandpa. You know what that means?" Jesse wasn't deterred by his grumblings, always chattering about this or that. "It means Santa will be here with toys even for the babies and no matter the big blizzard. Mama says Santa should have no trouble at all even if the train couldn't manage it."

Russ plopped a hand to his aching head but offered a smile to his grandson. Jesse had every right to be excited about the coming holiday, but he doubted much the twins, Ricky and Rusty would much care what Santa was bringing as long as they were fed on time. All those two babes at several months old did was fuss until they had a tit in their mouths. But he'd be lyin' if all three of his grandsons didn't tug at his heart strings.

Harold, Jesse's pet rooster, jumped to the foot of the bed and gave a loud coca-doodle-doo which pulled Russ right up to sitting. He gave the flocking creature a hard glare. "Good morning, Jesse and Harold." The rooster, Jesse's constant companion had been his idea a few years back and followed his grandson everywhere.

The smallest in the brood had caught up and was now better than any guard dog who patrolled the ranch announcing the arrival of anyone new.

"I put another wood in the fire on account it's cold in here and Pa said you were a sleepin' off another drunk," Jesse explained as he picked up the rooster and set him back to the floor.

Russ studied the boy for a long moment. "That what your Pa said?" He thought he'd made it to the bunkhouse unnoticed, but it seemed his son never missed a trick.

"Yep. Are you on another drunk, Grandpa?" The boy's deep brown eyes studied him, but his brows narrowed, waiting on an answer.

Russ nodded. Soon enough his son would show up and another lecture on his drinking would come.

He hadn't a doubt of that.

He ran a hand through his shaggy gray hair. It was cold and he tugged on his undershirt, pulling it over his head and pushing his arms through it. He worked his arms into his gray buttoned shirt and then plopped his hat on his head.

"Nah, Boy, not drunk no more. It's all slept off." It wasn't a lie as he hadn't imbibed since the night before, but it seemed a better thing to be truthful. It was clear Jesse had heard enough.

He had only his own ass to kick for that.

Jesse sat beside him with a pout. "Don't you love us, Grampa?"

"'Course I do." He patted the boy's thigh. Jesse was Laurel's son from her first marriage, but he'd found a fast friend in the little boy when they'd first met some time ago. And now, it was hard to remember that the boy wasn't his son's child, but that fact mattered little. Caleb was the only father the boy remembered anyway.

He took a good look at the boy, his heart softening. Jesse wore a heavy blue coat with silver buttons and a stocking cap to match his gloves. "But Pa says you drink too much and it's gonna kill ya. Grandpa. I don't want you to die."

He gave it some thought as he stretched his back and gave a yawn. "I ain't goin' nowhere yet, boy. Tell ya what. Bring me those saddle bags." Aiming for distraction was all he had not to answer this one. "Got ya some gumdrops from town though you just eat a few or that Mama of yours will have my hide."

Jesse grabbed the saddle bags with both hands and plopped it beside him. Russ dug inside and retrieved a paper sack of candy.

The boy grabbed it, shoving a gumdrop into his mouth. He slurped. "Thank you, Grandpa." He scampered toward the door with the sack but turned again and ran back to almost knock Russ over with a hug. And then like a flash he was gone, the rooster following with a flurry of feathers and squawks.

Russ chuckled and held his head with a grimace. He studied the saddle bags and pulled out the revolver he'd taken from inside Elliott Charles's hotel. He opened the weapon peering inside.

It still smelled of smoke. One chamber was empty while the other remained full. So, it had only taken one shot to do the deed.

Why? Charles had been in town before the train had derailed. And the man had been overly interested in his two cronies on that train, both having sustained little injury from what he'd seen.

He closed the barrel again and turned it back and forth. As fancy a small gun as he'd ever seen, more for show than for shooting.

He set the little gun aside and pulled the papers he'd lifted from the man's room and read the names again. DeWayne Jeffries and Ronald Glenn, neither of the names familiar. Elliott Charles had added his name to the others on an agreement which appeared to be some type of deed. Businessmen from New York was all he could figure there.

Well, that was telling in and of itself. Numbers of those from back East were always assuming they'd find a fine dollar out west somewhere.

But why had they joined Charles and what relationship had the three had with Clancy Willowby?

He shuffled through the papers again while Jesse sat quietly nearby.

"I see ya found your way home." Caleb stood in the door, cold winds whipping through as he eased it closed, but not all the way. "Where you been the last few days? Thought you were huffing mad…figured you at the saloon again."

"Seems you all but kicked me out in the blizzard." He grumbled back. "Though it's my own doing." He added as an afterthought.

Caleb nodded. "Uncle Russ…Pa…"

"Look, I need your help with something…you can lecture me later." He'd settled the demons of the night, the ones making him want the relief of a nip…and the faces of those who had brought him to it. And he wasn't going to lose Addie like he lost them…she wasn't gonna hang for murder, he'd make sure of it.

"Miss Addie?" Caleb angled a glance at him tilting his hat back. "I heard. Laurel and Leona are pretty upset, Leona's here to help with the babies this morning."

"Leona?" He stood and buttoned his shirt. "Dalton here?"

"He's got Sable in the barn." Caleb tossed a thumb over his shoulder. "Threw a shoe. Fixing it himself."

Russ fixed a gaze on his son again. "Addie's jailed but she didn't do it...got a few ideas but...get Dalton in here." The man was becoming right handy with the care of horses and things around his own ranch so that wasn't a surprise. The famous gambler had found his way once more by leaving the life behind and marrying Leona. Both of them lonely hearts who never needed love until it hit them.

Caleb moved aside and Dalton appeared in the doorway, then shut it behind them both, lifting his cane under his arm as he sat in one of the chairs.

"Ah, hell you can both save it." It took a moment for him to figure out that Caleb had talked to Dalton about his drinking and the two were about to spell it all out for him again.

"Just offering, but you gotta be the one who is ready..." Dalton rested both hands to his cane. The man's deep green eyes told the truth of it. He'd been there and knew all about leaving liquor behind.

Russ held up a hand. "You two can scheme my recovery later. I got a few irons in the fire and I need to get to the bottom of what happened with Addie for now."

"Pa, Dalton's kicked the drink, and he can help you do the same." Caleb narrowed a gaze on him shoving his hands into the pockets of his heavy coat.

"All right, all right but I need your help first for Addie." He shook his head. His drinking too much wasn't to be solved overnight and right now there was little time to save Addie.

"Leona's pretty upset." Dalton rubbed his bad knee, the chronic injury left over from a gunshot wound to the knee and a bad set of cards.

Russ nodded. "Branch has her holed up in the jail but she doesn't remember what happened. But...I got an inkling of a start to free her."

Folding both arms across his chest, Caleb shook his head. "We're not busting her out are we?"

Dalton chuckled under his breath. Both men knew him well enough not to put such an idea past him. It wasn't that he hadn't thought of it and already offered Addie an escape. But she wouldn't go for that, and the reality was Siberia was quite a long way and rather frozen. He'd meant that as a joke, but he wasn't finding much very funny. Adding to it, the headache gaining strength.

"Addie didn't do it," Dalton said. "I read faces, she's never held a guilty one."

"No but here's the gist." Russ glanced at each of them in turn. "Clancy Willowby, the man that was gutted in the alley, came to town a few days before saying he was taking over ownership of the social club."

"Ownership?" Caleb narrowed his brows and leaned on the table.

Russ tucked his shirt. "She was married to Farley Willowby when the social club was purchased. She wasn't aware he'd borrowed the money from his brother. But now the bastard's dead, but he didn't come to town alone. Got an Elliott Charles, some lawyer from Cheyenne, at least as best I can figure. Think he killed Clancy too and framed Addie."

"Top hat, hanging at the hotel?" Dalton angled a glance, leaning farther back into the chair as he asked.

"I saw him when the train derailed, looking for two men from New York. Seems they survived things fairly, both at the hotel with him," Russ added with a glance to Caleb. "I did some snooping in the hotel."

"You didn't." Caleb rolled his eyes. "Branch will haul you right in for that."

Russ smiled as he held up the derringer. "Never doubt me, boy." His son should know better, he didn't wait on the law when he needed answers. "This has an empty chamber and smells of a recent shot."

Caleb came closer to peer at the weapon. "One shot to whom?"

Russ chuckled. "Clancy. Seems Addie had gone to pay him off after he'd been to the Social Club. She doesn't remember anything, but later Eef found her in the snow unconscious, got her back and cleaned her up. She was covered in blood, but she wasn't injured."

"So, what are you thinking happened?" Caleb took up the gun and looked inside, sniffing.

"Later, he was found in that alley by the sawmill, stabbed multiple times, Branch has Addie's letter opener," Russ explained. "It was found near the body, so it was definitely used."

"So Charles got Willowby and dumped him in the alley," Dalton surmised, "before the train derailed, which would put him late to the scene. Somewhere along the way, Addie was left unconscious...and

Charles took her letter opener."

Russ held up the gun once more. "I'm not thinking Willowby died from stab wounds. But here's where I could use some help. I need you boys to distract Charles, keep an eye on him and his men while I take the Doc and Branch to look at Willowby's body."

Caleb shook his head. "That would explain the blood on Addie and maybe how he had her letter opener."

"Not sure how things happened, and Addie can't remember much, but I am banking on Clancy Willowby having a gunshot wound. It was a full blizzard, no one around, bastard somehow renders Addie unconscious, kills Clancy with the derringer, hauls him off and stabs him with her letter opener multiple times." He buckled his gun belt low around his hips. "Boys, I say we make a trek to town and free Addie of this whole thing."

Dalton gave a nod and stood, holding his cane to one side. "Nothing like the present."

Caleb shook his head. "Wait, you can't just go digging through those bodies."

"Says, who?" Russ shrugged his coat onto his shoulders. "If the Doc verifies Clancy was shot and we take Branch with us, mystery solved. But there's more."

Caleb kicked a boot to scuff the floor. "Well, Branch isn't gonna go for that at all. He'll arrest every one of us."

"If the Doc's there, Branch won't have legal reason to stop us, though he won't like it." Russ lifted his brows. "I got papers here where I can show Charles and these men have worked a deal for The Social Club, killing Clancy to get rid of him. No smarts there, but Doc found out the two men with Elliott, a Jeffries and

Glenn, have a long track record of smuggling."

Caleb exhaled a loud breath.

"I'm thinking the social club being near the rail is the only reason they want it. If these men are smugglers, opium, whiskey, and the like, they need that location." Russ smirked as he headed for the door. "Now, I promised my grandson I'd have a bit of breakfast with him. Soon as that's done, we can head into town and take care of business, boys."

It was Dalton who stepped before him, blocking his way, and lifting the brass end of his cane to stop him. "I can leave Leona here with Laurel, but there's still one thing."

Caleb turned saying nothing as did Russ.

Dalton lifted his cane and turned the brass end up and put it to Russ' shoulder. "I'm in, but I'm gonna need your word on something."

Russ looked down at the brass cane and back up.

"When this is over and spring arrives, you and I are taking a little trip for about three months to the hills here on the ranch, build a cabin for you and Miss Addie." Dalton winked. "Not taking no for an answer."

Well now, he'd got his hind end in a fine mess. He glanced from Dalton to his son and back, both men holding a grin. "I reckon I don't get to opt out of this one."

"Nope." Dalton shook his head back and forth and lifted the cane away with a smile. "Then let the games begin, after you, sir."

Caleb led the way back toward the house out in the weather as Dalton followed them both toward the house to breakfast. Russ mumbled a curse. Building a cabin was nothing but hard work and it would be hot and there would be no liquor to quench the ache or quiet the reasons he wanted it in the first place. But for Addie, he could damn well do anything he had to—including giving up the drink once and for all.

Chapter Fourteen

Wind whipped heavy and cold, though a hint of sun peeked through the clouds as Russ rode Diablo into town. Wylder was good and awake, though given the weather fewer people roamed the snow-piled streets, even though it was Christmas Eve.

Dalton and Caleb had made their way to the saloon to see if anything was going on with Charles and his cronies. His son had also let Doc Coyote know to find Branch and bring him to the isolated building behind the livery.

Inside his coat he carried the small derringer and the papers he'd lifted from Charles' room. He'd give those to Branch once he proved Willowby's frozen body carried a bullet hole. And then he could explain his theory on why the social club would come in handy if smuggling by rail. It should prove enough of the truth to free Addie from hanging. Something he wasn't going to let happen no matter.

He dismounted and tugged Diablo along, heading to the shed out back of the livery. In the distance, the tin roof stuck out like a sore thumb, the one building standing on its own and always locked up tight. Oh, it didn't belong to Chet Daniel's or the livery. It was owned by the township of Wylder, a place to store bodies when folks died in the dead of winter. Most of whom would be buried the following spring as soon as the ground thawed.

Clancy Willowby would be inside, as well as those who had died when the train derailed and some elderly from around the township who'd passed recently.

He lifted his pocket watch from inside his heavy coat. Half past ten. Good enough. He shoved it back into his vest pocket. Doc Coyote should join him in a bit, and the physician would be bringing Branch Wylder.

Branch was new to his job, a good lawman, if not one overwhelmed by the job and the chaos of the train wreck. In time he would make a right decent sheriff. His keeping Addie behind bars was because he had no other choice, given Addie's letter opener had been found beside Willowby's body. And here in a minute, if his suspicions were right, he'd have this whole thing resolved and drag Elliott Charles in right on his ass.

He waited outside the double doors of the shed. Death lingered along with the smell of manure and hay from the livery. Summer bodies weren't kept inside more than a day, but the reek then could be as bad as the trash pile that was burned each month outside of town.

He jiggled the lock. Ah, he could break in with ease, but Coyote would be here with the sheriff in a short time. He gave Diablo a pat and walked to tie the horse off to the corral fencing at the back of the livery. He grabbed the roping of his lasso and tossed it to sail across the air and then began coiling it with the precise turn in his grip that it wouldn't tangle. And he tasted what he wanted to do to Elliott Charles, but what he had in mind would keep him from his own noose. He chuckled. He'd bet the top hat fancy clad thief and cheat wouldn't have any idea what was about to hit him.

But it was the same for him of sorts. If this turned out like he thought, then he'd spend his spring breaking his back and drying out from the bourbon he craved at this moment. Just a sip…that would be good, but he pushed back the idea and studied his trembling hands. He didn't have much choice and for Addie he would do it, though there was no real guarantee she'd believe him once more enough to let him try. No, there was no try, there was do it or walk away from her forever because he'd never again be the reason she suffered a day of false hope. He'd dried out a time or two but never for long. He supposed if he could manage it under Dalton's supervision he'd make it but not before he cussed, whined, and begged.

He pulled his coat tighter and shook his head. If anyone could help him it would be Dalton. The gambler wasn't always so famous. Years ago his own drinking binge had caught him a bullet to his knee, and he's suffered the pain of it since, relying on a cane after multiple surgeries.

Now it was his turn. He'd do as he promised if he thought Addie would be waiting. He glanced across town. Even with the blizzard leaving piles of snow the town was decorated for Christmas with green wreaths and red ribbons and sparkling candles in every window. Come to think of it. It was morning of Christmas Eve, as good a day as any to free Addie.

Things having slipped right up on him except for the fact of his grandson Jesse's reminder. He still needed gifts for his family…and Addie, but at this point it would have to come later. Though he was about to give the Madam a rather good Christmas and in the distance the doc and Branch were walking his way. He hung the coiled rope back on the saddle horn, tying it off to Diablo. Then he walked to the door of the "dead shed" as the young boys in town often referred to it, teasing each other it was haunted.

Doc met his gaze and winked. Things were going as planned. "Russ."

Branch narrowed his brows, tilting back his hat. "Wait a minute, what's he doing here?"

"Like I told you. We're here to set the record straight for Addie. I want to see that body, and you'll need to see it as well for proof." Coyote nodded at the locked door. "Go on, open it."

"Russ, you know you've my respect and all, but I can't let either of you tamper with evidence." Branch shook his head. "I am sorry about it being Miss Addie, but I found her letter opener myself right beside the man."

"You shoved evidence in the outbuilding for winter, we'll be lucky the man's head doesn't fall right off." Russ grinned at Coyote and then focused a stern glance on the lawman. "Now open the door or I will, sheriff. If Clancy has a gunshot wound, it happened long before he was stabbed numbers of times."

"Branch, I need to see the body for medical and legal purposes," the Doc added. "You don't want to hang an innocent woman like Addie. If we find Clancy Willowby shot, I'll write up the report myself."

Branch considered them both and with a frown and pulled the ring of keys from his belt, fumbling to find the right one. "Probably gonna catch hell from the circuit judge when he arrives. Good thing he's delayed with the damn train derailing."

After several tries with various keys, the lock parted for Branch to remove the chain.

Russ grabbed the double doors and opened one, leaving the other closed. A rising stench of decaying bodies met them. While the bodies were wrapped and frozen, some still rotted from the inside out. Not so much a smell of rotting flesh as a smell of stale air and death.

Coyote moved ahead of them, glancing around. "Remember where you put Willowby?" The physician began sifting through the piled bodies. It was clear he was on a mission to free his mother-in-law from the fate she'd been assigned.

It took a moment for Branch to answer, his face as pale as the snow on the ground outside. "Ah...there...in the corner."

Russ lifted his brows and went opposite of Coyote to unwrap the head of the first big body. "No, train got this one."

He covered the face again. He wasn't at all sure what Willowby even looked like. He'd seen the man somewhere in the past, but he wouldn't have made a mental picture of him to keep for any reason.

Coyote glanced at another, replacing the wrap back around the face. "This one, too."

Russ picked another and two more before he found Willowby, the wraps as bloody as any. "Got him." He studied the purple frozen face with closed eyes and a bit of a smirk. "Huh."

"Branch, light a lamp and bring it over," Coyote spat as he helped to pull Willowby's body free of frozen blankets. Russ laid the body flat on the floor of the shanty, but the upper body was bent and laid off the ground, frozen in place.

"Hey now…you both know you can't harm the body or anything." Branch moved closer still covering his mouth and nose with a gloved hand. The young sheriff didn't look so good and kept a bit of distance.

"You found the letter opener beside Clancy here, right?" Russ spoke but didn't look up. "And I hear tell he was stabbed multiple times with it."

"Yes, and the letter opener had Addie's initials on it. Plus, he'd been to the social club. Look, Russ, I know it's not like Miss Addie, but what would you have me do? There were witnesses how he was found like that." Branch eased closer and peeked at the body, his face wrinkling into a frown.

"And how was that." Russ bent to a knee as Coyote helped uncover the body from the other side.

"Well, he was on his back, and I looked at his chest…stabbed ten times from the count I took," the sheriff explained and took another step back.

Coyote tilted his hat back. "Was there a lot of blood in the snow when you found him?"

Branch gave it some thought and then spoke. "Some, but…come to think of it, not a lot but it was all soaked into his clothes there and he was near to frozen already."

Willowby rolled free with a thud as Coyote pulled the wrap harder. The body was stiff as a railroad tie and his face was purple his hands frozen together, ropes holding his arms to his body and his legs tied at the ankles. The man's clothing did have blood stains but not as it would appear he'd bled to death. Russ fought with the shirt and vest and ripped it down the front to

143

show Willowby's chest with its multiple knife wounds. He then took off his own gloves and checked the man's frozen coat, vest, and shirt. "These are stabbed through as well."

"Let's check the neck and back." Coyote observed the man's torso and then grabbed the lantern from Branch and set it to the dirt floor. "Branch, did you check his back that night?"

The sheriff hesitated still holding a gloved hand over his mouth and nose. "Well, no, but I saw all those stab wounds there. Colder than hell from the blizzard blowin' and it was not long after the train derailed, taking me away from investigating further."

"Let's turn him." Russ pushed and the Doc pulled until Clancy Willowby gave a loud burp, air escaping the body as he fell to one side.

Branch turned on a dime and ran for the door coughing and gagging once he was outside the shanty.

Russ glanced back at Coyote who chuckled along with him. The doc traced a hand under Willowby's hair line. "Yep. You were right." He pulled a length of hair back and a small hole lay open behind the dead man's ear in the side of his neck.

"Branch, you all right?" Coyote called out to him. "Take a couple of deep breaths and come look. He's got a bullet wound to the head. Which is why you didn't find much blood on the body at the time."

Branch took a moment, coughing and spitting outside and then he ambled in pale as a ghost.

"Here." The doc touched the open hole sticking a finger inside and pressing deep. Bullet's too deep, frozen besides. "Hand me your knife, Russ."

Russ leaned up and pulled his knife from his belt

and the doctor dug into the wound and after a bit of manipulating pulled out a metal ball.

Coyote held up the metal bullet covered in frozen blood. "Got it."

With that Branch took off on a run and outside the shed gagging once again and falling to his knees outside the door.

Russ chuckled. "Guess our new sheriff's a little wet behind the ears."

Coyote began wrapping Clancy back up. "You called it right, Russ. I'll write the report out, turn it in. Should free Addie right up. I got the papers you found and will make sure the sheriff gets them once he perks back up."

Russ tugged the quilting back over Clancy's face. He'd been right. He and the doc lifted Willowby back to the pile of bodies.

"That should do it, Branch saw for himself." Russ followed the doc outside where Branch hung over the corral fencing near Diablo. The sheriff retched again.

Coyote laid a hand on his back. "Easy does it, Branch."

The sheriff wiped his mouth once again. "So, this proves Miss Addie's innocence but…who did this, that lawyer from Cheyenne?"

"Seems like I thought, Charles came to town with Clancy. He needed the deed that said the social club was his. But Clancy got in the way of the plan, I suppose. Addie wasn't remembering much. But when she was found unconscious, she was covered in blood that didn't belong to her. I'm sure Elliott Charles thought he might do away with her as well."

Russ nodded, untied Diablo, and continued.

"Clancy Willowby was dumped there in the alley, but Addie was found farther away. I got documents the doc can share with you for proof these men were banking on the social club being near the rail. A right fine place to smuggle goods all over the west. It all makes a perfect story, Sheriff."

Russ took a deep breath and let it out. He'd done it.

Coyote grabbed Branch by the arm. "Let's get you back. Slow deep breaths now."

"Doc...that body made a sound." Branch mumbled, but shook his head. "You ain't gonna tell anybody I got sick are ya?"

"Nope, not gonna say a word." Coyote shook his head. "Bodies get air trapped inside. Quite common to hear a gurgle or a burp or two."

Branch nodded, squeamish once more with a moan, holding his belly. "Russ...I'll come help."

Russ shook his head. "I've got this one, Sheriff. Be bringing him in shortly."

Coyote held his gaze. "Watch yourself, Holt."

Russ gave a nod and then mounted up on Diablo lifting the lasso and taking the horse toward the saloon on a canter, all he wanted out of the rest of his life, waiting ahead of him.

****

Russ glanced into the near noon sky. Gray and cold as hell but his mind...well, that was clear for the first time in a while. And he was about to do what needed done...whether Addie could find forgiveness for him or not. She'd be free now. Wasn't gonna hang like they all thought...but he hadn't been about to let that happen anyway.

Coyote headed back to the jail with a nauseated

Branch, and all the papers and proof would be documented on how Clancy Willowby had met his end. The social club would belong to Addie once more with his death regardless of deeds or claims to ownership.

He glanced at his hands. He needed no drink right now, the task at hand mapped out for his doing. He wasn't sure at all the skills a man like Elliott Charles, or his men would have, but he would be finding out. Once he hauled the man in to be jailed and made sure Addie was safe, he could celebrate Christmas with his grandsons…and he wasn't gonna wait until spring to start the building of that cabin with Dalton Payne. If he could get through a day at a time with no drink, he could go ahead and be cutting some of the lumber needed to build a fine home for him and Addie—she could forgive him and believe he would make a change.

He lifted his brows and shook his head. There were still no guarantees she'd be letting the past go and he'd disappointed her more than enough over the years. And she sure wouldn't be believing anything about him drying out until he'd done it.

He angled a glance across the frozen town. It was Christmas Eve and he'd a hell of a Merry Christmas for Elliott Charles and his men. He chuckled. It might be catching them by surprise to his advantage, but he had to be careful not to get himself, Caleb, or Dalton shot.

At the corner of the Five Star Saloon, Caleb leaned against the far wall and gave him a nod. On the roof of the adjacent building Dalton tipped his hat. So, as he thought Charles and his men were inside the saloon where they seemed to stay to do their bidding on smuggling he suspected. Well, that wasn't happening, and neither were a lot of things the man had up his sleeve.

As he rode closer, he had a good idea about what he was going to do to upset the plans Charles thought he'd already managed. He glanced at Caleb again and his son ambled off in appearance but would be making his way to the back to the Five Star from the other side of the building.

As for himself, he wasn't so worried about the two men from New York. He wanted Elliott Charles.

He dismounted and gave Diablo a good pat. "Gonna need your help here, boy. Got some oats waitin' for ya later."

He wrapped his left hand around the curled roping on the saddle horn and lifted it. For a long time now, he'd always rounded more rope than he needed but today it would serve its purpose. With his right hand he touched his revolver and then patted his breast pocket where the derringer he'd taken from Charles' room rested. He had plans for that too.

He took a deep breath and stepped inside the saloon. Sonny Cash gave him a nod. Caleb would have let the man know a bit of what was going to happen. Sonny would agree if it meant the Five Star wouldn't be damaged.

The saloon was filled with patrons, some sitting alone or standing at the bar, others playing cards. And at a table toward the windows was Charles and the two men with him, all involved in a poker game of five card draw. None of the men took notice of him and that was a good thing too.

He ambled to the bar, wanting that taste of bourbon to quench his nerves. He struck a match and took the small brown cigar Sonny offered him. The saloon owner then bent behind the bar and uncovered a shotgun, placing it to stand in the inside of the bar. The bartender wouldn't be in on details, but he could be counted on.

Russ nodded and inhaled and then blew out a puff of smoke. One for the long haul he supposed. But no liquor for this one. He puffed a few more times and put the smoke out in the tin cup and pulled off his coat, laying it over one of the stools, for the most part unnoticed.

He held the rope in his left hand and walked over to the table standing before Elliott Charles.

Charles looked up at him and back to the cards. "You opting into the game, sir?"

Russ eyed the two men from town who were in the game and gave each a nod. Both tossed their cards down and moved from the table, fully aware it was in their best interest to part with the game.

Charles folded his cards before setting them down. "We've had a real fine game going on. What business do you seek?"

One of the cronies chuckled. "Seriously, the drunk at the hotel? What'ya want, a handout? Here."

The man tossed a golden eagle his way. Russ caught it and slammed it onto the table. "All of you sit where you are. If you move, you're as good as dead." He didn't raise his voice but made things clear.

Silence filled the table, and the noise in the saloon lessened. He turned back to Charles. "Seems you came here with a man named Clancy Willowby to take over the social club as a partner. It's rather strange how the man wound up dead in an alley on the coldest night hell's ever seen. But did you realize on his untimely death, Addie Willowby is now the rightful owner of that Club?"

Charles postured, sitting stiff and his eyes narrowing to slits. "The woman killed him from my understanding with multiple stab wounds from her letter opener. At least, I heard that's what the sheriff found."

"Sheriff never said openly there was a letter opener involved." Russ eyed the other men who didn't move. "Check."

Charles chuckled. "Well, it's common knowledge the man was stabbed multiple times and I've heard inside this saloon what I just said. Wouldn't you agree, gentleman?" He waited on nods from his men.

"I suppose you wouldn't know a thing about Clancy Willowby meeting with a bullet before that letter opener was used then?" Russ added fuel to the fire.

The man loosened his collar and placed his hands to his knees. "I assure you I know nothing of the sort."

"Is that right?" Russ slammed the derringer that belonged to Charles on the table. "Seems your bid for the social club is now up."

One of the other men moved and Russ drew his revolver. "Go on, grab it."

No one moved as Caleb and Dalton walked through the front of the saloon weapons wielded. Behind them, Doc Coyote came through the curtain from the back storeroom, his revolver poised and at the bar Sonny wielded the shotgun.

"That's right. I got you all numbered. You two have a long line of history smuggling opium and whiskey. Just needed a place to store it all up in the social club…right near the tracks." He held Charles' gaze. "Run the town like you see fit…well this ain't your town. This is Wylder and your kind don't belong here. But…first things first. You're going to jail for the murder of Clancy Willowby in cold blood. And you two for aiding it all to happen."

Charles tried to stand up, but Russ used an elbow to knock him backwards to the floor. He then pushed to flip the table over on the other two who bobbled backwards in their chairs with a crash. Caleb and Dalton were on them in that brief second.

Before Charles could move farther Russ grabbed the man's booted right foot and pulled the end of the lasso tight around it and whistled.

Charles glanced as the uncoiling rope was being pulled from outside, but he couldn't know it was tied off to Diablo who'd just taken off on a run. The man's body shifted, and he was dragged on his back out of the saloon and onto the ice-covered ground.

Russ took off outside pushing through the men who watched. He whistled again and Diablo stopped, leaving Charles still on the piles of snow that had gathered underneath him.

Charles fought to free his leg, spitting and sputtering. "You can't do this. That woman killed him. Not me. That bitch."

Russ mounted up on the horse and urged him to a slow trot, dragging the squalling man behind him. Ah, it wasn't gonna hurt him because they wouldn't be going far. Russ turned the corner wide urging the horse ahead and making sure Charles' body cleared both corners as he made his way to the sheriff's office. A crowd followed as Charles cursed and raged yelping along the snow-covered frozen ground.

Russ stopped the horse, leaving Charles on his back in the street. A crowd began to gather around the side alleys and shops. He dismounted and walked over to Charles coiling the rope again and handing it off to Branch who was well passed his nausea.

"A cheat, a liar, a thief, and a murder all wrapped in one. Cheyenne, Wyoming bottom shelf."

Russ used the rope to pull Charles to his feet. The man was unsteady, whining and grumbling among his curses.

"Oh, quit your belly aching...you made this bed and now you can lie right in it." Russ gave the man a swift kick in the ass as Branch pulled the rope in to handle Elliott Charles.

Caleb rounded the corner, his own rope tied to the two smugglers from New York City. He tied them at the next jail post and gave his father a nod. Dalton followed after taking his place beside the Doc, both men smiling. They'd done it, all of them together.

But then Addie stepped to the doorway of the jail. She didn't say anything, but held his gaze as the entourage of ladies who loved her followed. Cornelia who had never learned the fine art to shut her mouth and Eef who gave Russ a smiling nod. The girls from the social club were clapping, the baby he'd rescued from the train wreck in Amethyst's arms. And behind them all was a group of nuns that had Addie plum stirred up with their continued presence in the club.

He stepped closer removing his hat as he held Addie's gaze. She was beautiful as always and the relief showed on her face though she was hard to read. What did he say now? It was sure a lot of things should be said. A lot of things he owed her to recover his good standing if it could be recovered.

"Russ…" she began but he interrupted.

"Wait. I got some things to say." He glanced around. Addie, his son, Dalton, the Doc, and Branch all right there along with the lingering crowd. Maybe it was that they all should hear him.

"I ain't give you or my son reason enough to believe I can let go of the whiskey. But I got a clear plan about it…if you're willin' to hear me out."

Addie glanced to Caleb and back.

"I've hidden a lot of pain in those bottles but…I almost lost everything once again. And I don't want to let that happen…so Addie if you'll do me the pleasure…" He bent to his knee. "I done asked you a bunch of times but I'm asking again, one last chance you might find it to believe in me."

Tears filled her eyes but didn't fall. Even Cornelia closed her mouth.

"Come spring, Dalton there and my boy are gonna help me build the best cabin this side of any town west. One you'd be proud of, and I won't be having no reasons for the bottle anymore. I never promised you that before, but I'm promising now."

"Russell…" Addie's voice cracked.

"Marry me, Addie. Leave the club for the ladies and the girls there. Give my heart a smile every day I draw breath." He gave her all he had, his own voice shaking in the truth of what he spoke.

But then she shook her head and his heart deflated two sizes. She was still done. Not going to accept what he offered. Well, he'd done all he could. He wouldn't beg, not like this in front of a crowd. He wouldn't bring any embarrassment on her. One thing he'd learned, when Addie made up her mind, it was for good.

He turned and began to walk back toward Diablo to all the whispering female voices behind him but then she spoke loud and clear.

"Russell Holt. Hold it right there."

He waited and then turned; uncertain his next breath of air was coming.

"Well, you barely gave me a minute to answer." She slammed her hands to her hips. "What makes you think I want a cabin on that ranch of yours out in the woods anyway?"

He wasn't sure her meaning, or if she was accepting of things. "'Cause we can sit on the porch and rock our grandchildren and dance by the hearth and…a lot of things."

"Why?" She lifted those brows making him wonder what the hell she was up to.

"Why?" he asked, perplexed.

"Yes, why?"

He shrugged. "It's what married people who love each other do."

She took a deep breath and let it out. "All right then."

"All right? You mean all right you'll dance by the hearth and bounce grandbabies on your knee?" He pushed, now he was sure she was giving the answer he wanted.

"Well, it would be a sight better than running away to Siberia or Mexico." She smiled then and something inside his heart relaxed.

Addie walked toward him, then broke into a run until she fell into his arms, He scooped her up, holding her as tight as he ever had.

"Yes, Russell Holt, I'll marry you. Now that I won't be meeting with a rope, I mean." With that her brave façade crumbled and she rested her face in his chest and burst into tears.

"Wasn't gonna let nothing happen to my Addie," he whispered. "Not ever. No need for tears." He pulled her back from him and brushed her cheeks with his thumbs and the girls and some of the town cheered and applauded.

"But I thought I was a goner. I really thought..." she bit her bottom lip and more tears escaped. "Thank you, Russ. I do love you and I'll be happy to have a real home and rock grandchildren with you. Wait a minute." She pulled back, her face serious, the pout he had come to love back in place. "You left me to sit in that jail, Russell Holt, and I am still angry for that."

He nodded and laughed. "Well, I said I'd take you to Siberia."

She giggled "No. I am not going to Siberia either."

"Well, how about Christmas in Wylder?" he asked.

"Now and forever," she added.

"Forever is a long time with a man like me." He bent and kissed her, then handed Diablo's reins to his son. Caleb gave him a smile and nod and his heart swelled in pride. He had a fine son and a good woman to love him. Things were exactly how they should be.

Caleb stepped up and took the horse. Merry Christmas, Pa. Merry Christmas, Miss Addie."

Russ scooped Addie up into his arms.

"Russ, what are you..." She wrapped her arms around his neck. "Russ, it's a long way to the club all the way across the tracks, you can't possibly..."

"I know but I got you back in my arms once more. Not about to put you down ever again." He began down the road toward The Wylder County Social Club. It was cold as hell, but he was as warm as he'd ever been with her in his arms.

"No, don't ever let me go again, Russell Holt." She leaned into his chest as she hung on. "And you can talk all night if you like. I promise I'll listen as long as it's you doin' the talkin'."

He growled and kissed her again. "Well now I wasn't planning too much on talking tonight.

"Oh. Well in that case walk a little faster." She giggled and whispered in his ear. "Merry Christmas, Russell Holt."

"Merry Christmas, Addie, always and forever."

Epilogue

Wylder, Wyoming
Ten years later

The sun hovered over the peaks of the mountains, glowing orange as it made its way down to the horizon.

The smell of fresh earth and the fragrance of early blooming flowers hung in the air. Addie closed her eyes and inhaled. Would she ever get used to this contented feeling? Russ had promised her they would have their own little haven, but even now, all these years later, there were times she had to pinch herself to make sure she wasn't dreaming.

The door groaned on its hinges as it opened and Russ stepped out onto the porch, carrying two steaming mugs of coffee.

He set one on the small table beside her and then took a seat in the rocking chair next to hers.

"Dinner was nice," he said, drawing her attention.

She couldn't help the smile that came over her. Dinner with their children and all the assorted grandchildren was one of her favorite things about their lives together—the combination of his son and her daughter and their spouses and offspring. They'd gathered at Caleb and Laurel's place and the rest had joined them.

Good food, good conversation, and lots of laughter. It was a life she'd never dared dream of for herself.

"Eef looks good." He brought his cup to his lips, casting a glance her direction as he did so.

Addie's heart warmed. "She sure does." Aoife had also joined them for dinner, along with her husband Cade. She'd inherited five grown children when she'd married the ranch foreman, and now had a whole passel of grandbabies to fuss over.

Russ stretched his long legs out in front of him and for a while they sat in quiet contentment, watching the sunset, and sipping their coffee.

It was strange, this contented feeling. She'd have never imagined it. When she and Russ had first married, she'd kept the social club and they'd made their marriage work around her job.

But after a while, dividing their lives between living in town and staying in their cabin in between times just didn't feel right. Wyoming was becoming a state and with that change businesses like The Wylder County Social Club were going to be outlawed.

She never had found anyone to replace Emerald once she and Abraham married. Then Opal and Pearl married off and Ruby soon after. Heck even her sister Cornelia had learned that in the west, even a plain ol' spinster could find herself pursued by a bunch of love-struck cowboys. She, too, had married.

The nuns who had been stranded at the club after the train derailment had stayed on in town. Eventually Amethyst—now Sister Mary Magdalena—joined them and little by little, her business got smaller. Soon it was just her, Ruby, and Abraham runnin' things. Other places like hers opened up as the town grew, and she had always known when to cut her losses.

Eliza Jane had been pestering her for years to make the club a home for wayward girls, and after a while, it just seemed the right time. She'd sold the business to the nuns, and it was now the Wylder County Orphanage. But it wasn't just for children, they took in abused wives, runaways, most anyone who needed shelter. Abraham stayed on to tend the building and keep trouble from the doorstep, and as Aoife slowed down with age, Emerald started helping with the cooking. Now the two helped the nuns run the place.

It had been ten years now. Times were changing and Wylder had changed right along with it.

As the last of the sun's light disappeared, Russ reached over to give her hand a squeeze. 'You 'bout ready for bed, Mrs. Holt?"

"Russ, layin' beside you and listenin' to your stories is the best part of my day."

He stroked the pad of his thumb over her knuckle and her heart gave a little thrill, like it always did when he touched her. "Wasn't plannin' on talking tonight."

"Is that right?" She lifted her brows. "Well. Then, what did you have in mind?"

"Come on, I'll show ya." With that he stood and held out a hand to her and she took it as she had for the last ten years when the mood struck them both.

Happiness was what you made it and they had made that together, hadn't they? Russ hadn't had a single drop of alcohol in years now and the dreams and losses of his past had remained quiet.

For that she was thankful. Having Russ beside her forever was enough to make each day worth living.

Nicole McCaffrey and Kim Turner

A word about the author...

Nicole McCaffrey grew up watching *Wagon Train* and lots of old John Wayne movies with her grandma. She is pretty sure her love of the West began with those Saturday morning reruns. She has been writing most of her life and published her first story in 2006. She has been married to her best friend, Peter, for 25 years and together they have raised two amazing sons. When not writing she can be found gardening, reading, or spoiling her two rescue kitties.

~

Kim Turner writes western historical romance discovering her passion of writing at the age of eight. Kim graduated with a Bachelor's of Science in Nursing and holds a Master's Degree in Adult Education. Working as a registered nurse educator for over thirty years, she enjoys studying the medical treatments of the Old West as well as keeping up with the latest western movies and television series. While she loves reading anything from highlanders to pirates, she claims to have an unquenchable thirst for the American Cowboy when choosing her reads. Kim lives south of Atlanta with her husband and calls her greatest accomplishment the birth of one daughter and the adoption of another from China—neither of which came easy. Kim is a member of Romance Writers of America and Georgia Romance Writers. Kim's Motto: It's All About a Cowboy and the Woman He Loves...